Totally Bound Publishing books by Beth D. Carter:

Mad Delights

Red Wolves Motorcycle Club
Along Came Merrie
True North
When Dove Cries
Lily Roar

I0571291

MAD DELIGHTS

BETH D. CARTER

Mad Delights
ISBN # 978-1-78430-700-4
©Copyright Beth D. Carter 2015
Cover Art by Posh Gosh ©Copyright August 2015
Interior text design by Claire Siemaszkiewicz
Totally Bound Publishing

Published in 2015 by Totally Bound Publishing, Newland House, The Point, Weaver Road, Lincoln, LN6 3QN, United Kingdom.

Totally Bound Publishing is a subsidiary of Totally Entwined Group Limited.

MAD DELIGHTS

Dedication

I have to give this one to my editor, Faith. Without her saying, "You got another one in ya?" I never would've dreamed up Chloe, and, I must say, she and Faith are pretty awesome.

Also, a special big thanks to CR Moss. She is, without doubt, the best cheerleader a writer and friend can have.

Ek elska þik, Eiríkr hinn rauði. Someday I will write about Eric the Red.

Chapter One

Romeo stood alone in the club's chapel staring at the tainted chair that Shepard had corrupted when he'd sat in it as President. Much like the club, the piece of furniture had a dirty air about it that reeked of greed. He wanted to burn the damn thing, or take an ax to it. Shepard was dead, but that didn't stop the self-loathing pumping through Romeo every time he remembered Shepard's smug face. He'd known the bastard was the wrong leader for the club, yet he had accepted the VP patch and decided to drown the bad vibes in drink, drugs and pussy.

He ran his fingers over the large, oval table made of polished concrete that symbolized the unity of what the club should be. There was no fucking way to move it except by a crane. Wheels had always joked that it was their own version of the Round Table, taken from the mythology of King Arthur, and just like the legendary king, this table had its own share of treachery. Romeo had been with the club since he was thirteen, when Wheels had taken him under his wing to raise him as his own. The old biker had made sure

Romeo could take apart an engine and put it back together, had taught him how to shoot straight but keep his nose clean. And, above all, Romeo had learned about loyalty.

The Men of Hell now seemed to lack that basic yet utterly important quality. Other than Dax, his best friend and the enforcer of the club, he didn't know whom to trust. So many issues needed to be addressed. He hadn't a clue where to start, although the logical place would be weeding out those still loyal to Shepard's memory. Some of Shepard's followers had left, some had sworn they didn't know about his double cross or how he'd stolen money from the club. Some still stuck around.

"You okay?"

Romeo jerked out of his morose thoughts and turned to see Daxton Squire standing in the doorway with his hands on his hips. They'd been through a lot of shit together. He hoped this brewing storm would simply be rocky waves they could ride out.

"Yeah," he replied. "I'm trying to come to terms with the realization that Shepard wasn't working alone. I know of at least one brother who had to be in on his trafficking operation."

Dax sighed and Romeo saw his own feeling of resentment mirrored in his friend's dark gaze.

"I know. I came to the same conclusion."

"Either the books were doctored or there were two sets, I'm not sure which. And we have no clue as to how many others were involved."

"A Ponzi scheme turned sour," Dax said. He pushed his tall, muscular body from the doorframe and took his seat at the table. "You gonna sit?"

"Eventually. I just… It feels weird for me to sit in the chair, you know?"

"You belong in that chair," Dax insisted. "You should've had it when Wheels decided to step down."

"Maybe." Romeo ran his fingers through his long hair. *Guess it's time for a trim.* "I suppose I thought Wheels would be around forever. Stupid of me, or what?"

Dax shook his head. "No. Not stupid. I always thought he'd be around too, but that's what kids think, Rome, that life is forever."

"I didn't want this shit." He bowed his head. "This...responsibility."

Dax tapped a finger for emphasis on the table. "Wheels told me you had the most level head out of all of us. If anybody is fit to lead the Men of Hell, you are."

"Bullshit," Romeo spat. "If that were true, then I wouldn't have let Shepard spout his pretty little lies and convince those men out there of something better. I wouldn't have been happy with the VP patch. I wouldn't have drowned myself in fucked-up vices to cope."

Dax opened his mouth to fire back, but Romeo waved off the argument. No, he didn't need Dax to blow smoke up his ass. He knew his faults were glaringly obvious—at least in his eyes. Doubts crept into his mind now as he tried to figure out just what to do about the disloyalty inside the club. Shepard's supporters still grumbled the old president's name when they thought Romeo couldn't hear. In those moments, he wanted to let his rage out, but he knew bashing heads wasn't the answer. Yet he couldn't be soft, else he'd lose the tentative grip he had on the club.

Other fully patched-in members entered the church and took their places around the concrete table. His

VP, Boone Tempest, was the oldest member of the club, now that Shepard was dead, and that was the only reason he'd asked the man to be his right hand. Boone was a decent enough guy, big with sharp eyes that seemed to see everything. His ever-present shadow, Gabby Dixon, followed behind him. The man's real name was Gordon, but he rarely ever said a word. Wheels had given him the ironic moniker of Gabby way back when, and the name had stuck. A scar ran from his temple to chin, but he never talked about it. The only thing Romeo understood was that the only person who knew anything substantial about the man was Boone. Romeo didn't pry. Shit, they all had personal secrets.

The patched-in members allowed to sit at the table were from all walks of life. The MOH Bair chapter didn't discriminate. Burrito was Hispanic, Sioux was Native American and Hook was African American. Romeo didn't care about the color of a man's skin. It was a person's integrity that counted. His gaze lingered on the club accountant, Cipher. It was time that fundamental principle was made crystal clear.

The Brothers were quiet, and Romeo missed the joking and jostling from days gone by, when they'd had nothing else to worry about except the next drug run. When the last Brother had settled and looked toward him, he reluctantly sat in the goddamn chair and banged the gavel.

"There are some pressing issues we need to deal with," he began. He glanced at each man, meeting their stares head on. "Obviously, we need to find a new supplier. This club is flat broke. The only thing keeping us alive is the whorehouse, so unless someone can cough up the money Shepard stole, we need some fast cash soon."

He took a mental note of the glowers he received from Drifter and Bandit when he mentioned Shepard's crime. Two more Shepard holdouts he put on his list.

"I might know of a crack and snow source," Boone, the vice president, said. "Believe it or not, from Canada. Straight up Interstate 29."

"Convenient," Dax murmured. "We could get cheap Viagra while we're up there."

The men laughed.

Romeo held up a hand, silencing them all in an instant. "Who?"

"A man calling himself Red Eye. It's not meth, but I've heard his stuff is good, and the word is that he's looking for a new distributing partnership."

Romeo frowned. Could they be that lucky? "Sounds too good to be true."

"That's why we need to move now," Boone replied. "If we get his shit, then we can blow the Shanks away. It's far superior to the stuff they're peddling."

"Whatever drug we run, we don't use it," Romeo reminded him. "I don't want the Men of Hell turning into fucking junkies, got it?"

The spot between Boone's eyes creased as he frowned. "Of course."

Romeo relaxed and nodded. "All right. You'll follow up with this Red Eye?"

"Yes."

"Okay," Romeo said. "All those in favor?"

A chorus of ayes rang through the large, paneled room.

"Passed," Romeo said. "Now, the next thing I must bring up is Shepard."

He took notice of the way Drifter and Bandit stiffened, but they weren't the fish he was after. Right now, he wanted the person who had helped in nearly leveling his club to the ground.

"Cipher," Romeo said, singling out the only biker at the table who didn't ride often.

The man preferred to stay behind his desk, sorting numbers. His bald, tatted head clashed with the image of his thick-framed glasses, and he also had the muscle tone more suited to someone of his numerical profession.

"Boss?" Cipher questioned, hesitantly.

"I still find it extremely difficult to believe that, as the treasurer, you had no idea that Shepard wasn't channeling the money from the meth runs back into the club bank."

Cipher looked around the table. Sweat broke out on his upper lip as he met each gaze. "How was I to know? He told me there weren't any funds to deposit."

"So you thought he was making these runs out of the goodness of his heart?"

The members chuckled at the obvious sarcasm in his words, but Romeo ignored them to focus on Cipher's tells. For a numbers man, he sure was lousy at poker.

Cipher looked around wildly and his hand shook. "I thought he was breaking even."

"Breaking even?" Romeo surged to his feet.

Cipher flinched and flickered a quick, desperate look at the door. It was then that Romeo knew for certain the accountant wasn't playing legit or being truthful with him.

"About one point six trillion dollars is laundered a year through drug trafficking, and you simply thought Shepard's runs were coming up with nothing profitable?"

He took his time to walk around the oval cement table, walking by each Brother one by one. Cipher watched him with wide eyes until he passed behind him. Romeo stopped and looked down at the man's balding head and disgust filled him, leaving a sour taste in his mouth.

"Hell, we used to make a nice little profit off marijuana back when it was still hip and cool, but Colorado fucked that trade route up for us, so we turned to meth. So, Cipher, I'm stymied on how someone so knowledgable with the books could possibly be so dumb to think I wouldn't figure out you were working with him."

"No!"

Cipher tried to stand, but Romeo slapped his hand against the back of Cipher's head and smashed his face into the table. Romeo held Cipher down while he struggled to free himself from the vulnerable position, but Romeo had a lot more muscle on him. He kept the fucking traitor easily in place.

"This is going to be a new club and I'm not a fucking nice guy anymore." Romeo looked around to each member of the table. "If I learn you've disrespected the patch on your cut or have been disloyal to this club, I will cut off your balls and stuff them down your throat, before I put a bullet in your head. Understand?"

Each man nodded to his warning–even Drifter and Bandit, although Romeo still reserved judgment as to whether they were simply playing along or if they truly agreed.

"Dax, take Cipher to the garage. Secure him to one of the cherry pickers."

Dax stood and obeyed without question. He grabbed Cipher's arms and marched him out of the chapel. Romeo gripped the back of the chair he hated so much and lifted it, bringing it with him as he followed Dax and Cipher. Slowly, one by one, each Brother trailed after him, and the other members and club whores hanging out in the clubhouse made room as they marched single file outside. They formed a parade line to the garage.

When Romeo arrived at the open work bay, Cipher was bound to the cherry picker. His hands were chained over his head, and the tips of his shoes barely scraped the ground. Terror blanketed his face.

"Please, boss," he begged.

"Please what?" he asked.

Cipher stared at him. His mouth quivered just a little. "I thought I had to be loyal to Shepard."

"Shut up," Romeo ordered coldly. He set the chair down and turned to look at the men behind him. "From now on, this club is about loyalty to the patch, no matter who sits at the head of the table. Understood?"

Once again, every man nodded.

Romeo pulled out the fifteen-inch, double-edged switchblade he never went anywhere without. He sliced away Cipher's cut and T-shirt to reveal his club tattoo on the right shoulder blade.

He looked at Dax. "Hold him."

Dax put his arms around the thinner man and held on while Romeo brought his knife down to slice into the skin. Cipher screamed until Boone stepped forward and stuffed a bandana into his mouth. Still, through the cloth, he continued to howl. Tears coursed down his cheeks. Romeo didn't give a flying fuck. He cut away the tattoo in a circular pattern, ignoring the blood that poured down Cipher's back, the sharp blade peeling the flesh like going through butter. When he severed the last bit, he stepped back and held the bloody disc of skin up for all the members to see. Cipher finally stopped screaming, so he figured the man had passed out.

"Traitors won't have the luxury of blackening out their tattoos. I will cut them from their bodies, however big they may be."

He walked over to the chair and put the tattoo on the seat. Dax handed him a shop rag so he could wipe his red-soaked hands as clean as he could get them before pulling a name patch from his pocket. Broken threads outlined the rectangular piece of material and Romeo sneered at Shepard's name embroidered on it. He spat on it then tossed it on top of Cipher's dissected skin. Next, he grabbed a can of gasoline and poured it over the chair and its contents.

"Burn it," he told Dax.

Dax pulled his lighter out of his pants pocket, set another shop rag on fire then tossed it on the chair. It lit up with a roar.

"Make sure he never steps foot in Nebraska again," Romeo said and walked away without a backward glance. "I need a new fucking chair."

Chapter Two

"You've had impressive surgical training, Miss Matsumoto," stated the voice through the computer's speakers. "But I have to warn you that Bair, Nebraska, isn't exactly a hip, happening place for a young woman."

Chloe gritted her teeth, but kept her smile over Skype. She wanted this job more than anything, and telling the surgical director of the very small hospital to go fuck himself wouldn't win her any brownie points.

"I've done extensive research on your hospital and on Bair, and your trauma rate is what appeals to me," she answered.

The director, Mr. Browning, sighed. "Yes, well, I should be brutally honest with you. Our trauma rate is mainly due to the motorcycle club getting into conflicts with the local drug gang."

"The Men of Hell, correct? And the Shanks?"

Even on the slightly distorted video, admiration shone on his face. "You *have* been doing your homework. Tell me, Miss Matsumoto, why would you choose to come to our very small hospital when you have the pick of top-notch hospitals in the country? Traveling surgical technicians can make a lot more money."

"I've worked in top-notch hospitals, Mr. Browning, and with all due respect to their reputations, it comes down to bureaucracy and less about patient care. My surgical training was basically an assembly line with a twenty minute turnaround time to sterilize the OR and prep for the next surgery. It may sound very cliché, but I'm looking for an environment where I can make a difference."

"Well, I can certainly give you that here at Bair Memorial," Mr. Browning said wryly.

For the next half hour, he managed to grill her on the different procedures she'd assisted in, bringing into call her textbook training and even some of the things she'd had to learn off the cuff. When the Skype interview completed, Chloe sat back, relaxed and, breathing easy, touched her fingertips together. She was positive she'd hear from Mr. Browning soon with an offer of employment.

"Wow," her friend, Clement, said from the kitchen. She suckled loudly on a Popsicle. "I almost believed that load of crap."

Chloe shrugged and closed the lid on her laptop. "Interviews are easy. You just have to tell them what they want to hear."

"Are you sure this is a wise move, Chloe? After, you know…"

"Don't," Chloe ordered stiffly. "Don't go there. It's over and I'm not in jail. Let's leave it at that." She loved Clement dearly, but it was always the same with her—the doubt and uncertainty shining brightly in her eyes. Of course, it didn't help matters much whenever Chloe went off on a tangent. "Besides, it's different this time."

"How?" Clement asked skeptically.

"Well, for one — do you see any photos on the walls?" Chloe gestured around the room.

Clement shook her head. "No. But this move does have to do with Kaiya's abduction, doesn't it? You've not been the same since she came back."

"Partly," Chloe said with a shrug. "I have a life debt I must repay."

"There is no such thing as a life debt," Clement said dryly. "That was a term made up for plot ideas in books and movies."

"For me, it's real," Chloe said. Her thoughts briefly touched on her cousin, Kaiya. "Now stop, I want to be excited about getting this position."

Clement frowned. "But Nebraska? I can't imagine there's anything to do there. I'd miss Los Angeles too much. And you know your grandfather *will* come after you, when he figures out where you went."

"If he questions you, give him the letter I wrote. You have it, right?"

"Yep. Absolving me of all knowledge."

"Don't be afraid to use it," Chloe said. "My grandfather is the type of man you want to avoid pissing off."

Clement snorted. "Yeah, I know." She took Chloe's hand and squeezed. "I'll miss you, you know."

Chloe's heart lurched. Clement had been her one true friend, the only one to stick by her when she was hospitalized. "I know," she whispered. "I'm going to miss you too."

Clement took a step closer and cupped her face. "I wouldn't mind your obsessive love."

"God, I *hate* that word," she muttered. "I don't have obsessions. I have tangents."

"Your last *tangent* not only got you fired, you were almost arrested and it brought your grandfather back into your life. If you had just loved me, I would've put up with any of your irregular behaviors."

Chloe sadly shook her head. "That would make sense, but, unfortunately, I just don't find you sexually attractive, even though you are gorgeous."

Truer words had never been spoken. Clement was the complete opposite of her, with long blonde hair and sky-blue eyes, the epitome of a California girl. They'd been friends through high school and both had entered vocational college together, where Clement had finally come clean about loving pussy instead of dick. She'd wanted to have a relationship with Chloe, but after one night of awkward sex, Chloe had realized she definitely preferred cock.

"Don't sell yourself short," Clement murmured. She bent and kissed Chloe on the mouth. Chloe allowed it, knowing her friend wouldn't push for more, and soon Clement pulled back with a long, dramatic sigh. "Damn it, *why* can't you be a lesbian?"

Chloe patted her hand consolingly. "I'm sorry. Since you're so into the fish smell, how about we get sushi? My treat."

"You're such an ass sometimes," Clement said with a snort. "Okay, sushi it is. You'd better get your fill here, because I have a feeling Bum Fucked Bair, Nebraska, doesn't have too much fresh sashimi."

* * * *

Two days later, Chloe received the call, and the next day, she went about packing up her efficiency apartment to make the move to Nebraska. Satisfaction consumed her and part of the itch inside her had been scratched. She walked over to her closet and opened the door to stare at the mural on the wall. Varied pictures crowded the small corkboard, one on top of the other. She was going to have to buy a bigger board.

One man decorated the entire surface. Dark hair, piercing blue eyes... He stared at her from the shiny surfaces of the glossy four-by-sevens. She smiled, kissed her fingertips, and pressed them lightly to the man's photo. They were from her grandfather's personal files, from when he'd had Kaiya's rescuers investigated. As soon as Chloe had set eyes on the dark-haired man with a lady-killer smile, lustful possession had surged within her. She had to have him. Her pussy had instantly slicked, followed by an ache settling deep inside that only his cock could satisfy. She'd taken the photos and used them for masturbation fantasies. Her shrink liked to use the word 'obsessive' so she went along with everything he'd said, because it had been a condition of her grandfather, and she'd pretended to take the pills prescribed. But no one understood her—not Clement and certainly not her fucked-up family.

Except for Kaiya. Her cousin was the one good thing in her world, the only person who didn't hold any judgment against her for what had happened in her past or what the consequences had wrought. When Kaiya had been taken, it had been a week of pure hell for Chloe until they'd all learned Kaiya had been rescued. Romeo Barrigan had saved Kaiya, and, now, Chloe was determined to help him somehow.

She carefully took her little shrine down and packed it away in a box. When she was done sealing it, she stacked it with the other boxes that would arrive at her new home next week. In the meantime, she would have to get new pictures of Romeo Barrigan. She placed her camera bag beside her travel case and took one last look around her now bare apartment. Bair, Nebraska, waited for her. And so did Romeo.

He just didn't know it yet.

Chapter Three

Two weeks later...

"Final tally is good, Doctor Pinder," Chloe said from behind her mask. Even though it wasn't an open procedure, she still needed to verify that all the surgical items were accounted for. Laparoscopic surgeries were her favorite simply because she didn't have to worry too much about lost instruments or sponges within the body cavity.

"Excellent," the doctor replied. "I think we've now removed every gall bladder in Bair and the surrounding communities."

"I still have mine," she said teasingly.

"Hang out in enough restaurants around here and all the greasy food will certainly put you on my operating table."

Chloe chuckled. "No thanks. I like my gall bladder right where it is."

He handed her the trocar devices that punctured the abdomen for the surgery, and she placed them on the back table. The patient's belly was slowly deflating since the carbon dioxide wasn't being pumped in any longer.

"Will you glue the holes shut and add bandages?" the doctor asked her.

"Of course."

"Perfect. In that case, I'm out of here." The doctor stepped back from the OR table where the unconscious patient slept. The anesthesiologist waved him off while Chloe stepped up to use bonding glue to seal the puncture wounds. Minutes later, she was pulling off her surgical gown and loading up the surgical cart to haul the used instruments back to sterile processing.

"Done for the day?" Susan, the OR nurse, asked.

There was something about Susan that Chloe didn't like. Maybe it was the woman's narrow eyes where a deep divot between them gave her a perpetual frown. Maybe it was the highbrow tone she always used whenever she was talking to anyone she felt was inferior to her status as a nurse—like a surgical technician, for example. Chloe had dealt with her share of uptight nurses, and Susan seemed to be the type of woman who always judged on aesthetics. Chloe detested self-righteous cunts.

"Yes," she answered succinctly. Her brain was telling her to ignore the woman and move on. She couldn't do anything to jeopardize her position.

"Since tomorrow's Saturday, why don't we head out for some drinks together?" Susan suggested. She looked Chloe up and down, a pretentious smirk lifting the corners of her mouth. "You should head to my neck of the woods since there's no decent place in this town."

Chloe cocked her head. "I thought Bair was a town full of bars."

Susan sniffed. "Bars that have the lowest life forms on earth inside them. Puh-leaze. I mean, granted, those lowlifes give us work, but people like us don't need to associate at their level."

"People like us?"

"Educated people," Susan replied. "I live an hour north of here." She lifted her hand to her mouth to talk behind it, as if to keep a monumental secret. "It has a country club and I'm a member."

"You drive two hours a day just for work? I thought people only did that in areas like LA, to make the traffic even more horrendous."

Susan shrugged. "They pay more money here in Bair because they're desperate for an excellent-trained staff. The drug dealers and the nasty motorcycle club have kept this hospital in turnover hell."

Chloe's protective instincts came roaring to the surface. Romeo was president of the motorcycle club and hearing this bitch talk down about him had her fighting her natural instinct to walk over and slap the smirk off her face. To get her surgical certification, Chloe had taken an oath not to harm patients, but that didn't include knocking sharp-tongued shrews down a peg or two. She breathed through the beat-down inclination, but in the back of her mind, she'd already decided Susan had a target on her back.

"I've already got plans tonight," Chloe murmured.

"Oh," Susan replied. Her chin went up a notch, pushing her nose somewhere into orbit. "Well, maybe some other time."

"Maybe." Chloe would rather shove a red-hot poker in her eye than go out for drinks with Susan.

She walked away quickly, before her anger got the better of her, and wheeled the used cart to sterile processing. Then she headed to the locker room, where she showered and donned black jeans and a black shirt. She parted her straight obsidian hair down the middle and made two Scary Spice hair horns on her head.

Surprised looks followed her out of the hospital. For the past week, she'd gone home looking like she'd come to work, drab and professional. But Friday nights were different. On Friday nights, Romeo drove to the Whiskey Lick Her Bar, and tonight she planned to get plenty of pictures to hang on her wall. She hadn't seen him in a week, although she'd driven by the MC compound more times than she wanted to admit. She desperately needed her sexual fix. Masturbation simply wasn't the same without seeing his face as she fucked herself with a vibrating pink cock. Soon, she hoped to replace the fake cock with the real thing once he realized he needed her as much as she needed him.

A little voice of reason tried to break in through her focus. This was crazy, stalking such a man. Stalking *any* man, for that matter. True, she'd had problems in the past separating simple desire for love, but this was different. Her shrink would tell her she was obsessing once more, using that word she hated. He'd try to put her on pills again. And perhaps she *was* going a little crazy, but the goddamn shrink didn't know what she'd lived through. No one did except for her grandfather and Kaiya. Motorcycle gangs hadn't even been on her radar until her cousin had been rescued by one, then she suddenly knew where she belonged. Away from Los Angeles and the reminders. Away from her grandfather's business. *This* was where she needed to be.

Psychiatrists might call it obsessive. The world would certainly call her insane, but her life had never been normal and it never would be. Nothing was normal for a girl who had to kill her mother when she was only thirteen years old.

* * * *

There's that car again.

Right away, Dax had spotted it across the street as he, Romeo and two others drove up to the Whiskey Lick Her Bar, the hangout they came to every Friday night. They owned it and needed to collect the profits. It was the only source of income the club had right now, so it behove them to sit, drink and pretend to be merry.

Over the past several days, he'd seen the car outside the compound. It wasn't hard to miss because there weren't many Mercedes in Bair. The tinted windows prevented him from seeing the driver, but Dax suspected it was the Shanks spying on them. The gang operated all over the Midwest, from Arkansas up through Iowa. They'd slowly been infiltrating their drugs into the MOH territory, but they were small and poorly managed. The Mercedes, however, worried him.

He tensed as the sensation of being watched stole over him. He might not be able to see the person who stared at him, but he felt the inspection nonetheless.

"Coming, Dax?" Romeo called.

He glanced behind him and nodded to his club president. As always, a measure of guilt washed over him. He'd let his duties as an enforcer slide with Shepard, and the man had turned out to be a fucking psychopath with delusions of grandeur. He wouldn't slip again. When he looked back, he watched the car drive away, nothing but tail lights in the night.

"Yeah," he said. He turned and followed Romeo into the dark bar. Posh it wasn't. The sticky floor kept sucking at his shoes. The low lighting forced him to squint, the band sucked, and the drinks were barely chilled. But the girls were smoking hot. The Whiskey Lick Her was located right off the interstate and the flashing neon sign that read *A Lot of Girls* was a magnet for truckers. The Men of Hell made a nice little profit, and, in return, they provided muscle and protection for the whores.

The manager, Creole Jack, greeted them with a nod toward the back room. He and Romeo headed there immediately while the other Brothers, Babyface and Hawg, took up position outside the door. A minute later, Creole Jack entered with a towel draped over his shoulder.

"Let me open this safe and I got your money here waitin'," he said. His accent was thicker than his mud-like coffee. "You know, I had two men come in here the other day, askin' about y'all."

"Shanks?" Romeo asked.

Creole Jack shook his head. He'd moved to Bair back in the seventies, leaving his home state of Louisiana behind. The darkness of his skin made the whites of his eyes stand out in stark relief. He pulled out a red money bag and handed it over. Romeo unzipped it, thumbed through the stack of twenties and nodded in satisfaction.

"No, weren't no cops neither," Creole Jack said. "They weren't wearing cuts but they smelled like leather and they looked like bikers."

"What questions did they ask?" Dax asked.

"Askin' about the town. About you. They were real curious about the feud between you and the Shanks."

Romeo folded his arms across his chest. "What'd you say?"

"I told 'em I was just a manager." Creole Jack shrugged. "Told 'em I didn't know nothin' about the Men of Hell."

"All right," Romeo said. "If you see them again, call me."

"Of course," Creole Jack said.

"Would you give us a minute, Jack?" Romeo asked. Creole Jack nodded and left the room, closing the office door behind him with a soft click. "What's up?"

"There's been a Mercedes following us," Dax remarked.

"Then that leaves the Shanks out. No one in their organization drives one of those cars. So who the fuck is tailing us?"

"I don't know." Dax held out his hand. "I don't like it. Give me the money bag and I'll take it straight to the club."

"But I'm the one that takes it—"

"We need to change up your routine," Dax told him. "You've become a little predictable."

"You think that's necessary?"

"I do. So let me run it back to the club and you go find a way to let off a little of that restlessness you've had for a while. I'll be gone twenty or thirty minutes, tops."

"We should go together."

"I'll be fine," Dax insisted. "Change up your Friday night, okay?"

Romeo frowned, but he handed over the red money bag. Dax shoved it into his cut's inner pocket and held up his fist. Romeo bumped it with his own.

"See you in a bit," he said.

"I'll probably be in the back."

Translation—he'd be with the whores.

Dax left the office and made his way from the bar. As he stepped outside, away from the hazy atmosphere of the bar, he took a deep breath. Smoking was one thing he'd never really gotten into, although he did enjoy a joint every now and then. In his youth, he and Romeo had spent many a night getting high in the club's basement, but when he'd become the enforcer, he'd tried not to indulge too much.

He strapped on his helmet and turned on his bike. Almost immediately, he spotted the Mercedes cruising by and all types of warning hackles rose to the surface. Without another thought, he took off after the car.

Romeo watched Dax leave the bar then glanced over at the two prospects waiting for his orders. Although Babyface looked like he was twelve, he was in his early twenties.

"Catch up with him, make sure he makes it to the compound okay."

Babyface nodded and headed after Dax.

Romeo slapped Hawg on the shoulder and grinned. "Ready for some pussy?"

"Oh yeah, boss," Hawg replied.

The two men made their way into the back where the whorehouse operated. Two of his men, Hook and Wrench, stood guard, making sure no one messed with the girls. Candy Box, the madam, smiled widely when she laid eyes on Romeo. The woman was in her mid-forties with bubblegum-pink hair, blue eyes, and breasts that entered a room a whole minute before the rest of her did.

"Well, hello, you two handsome men," she gushed as she moved from behind her booking station to give each man a hug.

"Hi, Candy," Romeo replied with a wide smile. *Nothing quite like having huge tits pressed against my chest.* As he mused about them, he realized his mood had already improved.

"How may I help you, dears?" Candy asked, winking.

"Oh, Candy, if only you were still passing out your favors," Romeo teased back.

"You, sweetheart, could tempt a nun out of her knickers." Candy giggled, ad moved back to her station then glanced down at her book. "What tickles your fancy this evening? I have five girls ready to play."

Romeo glanced at Hawg questioningly. Hawg shrugged.

"Whoever's available," Romeo replied.

"Very well," she said and texted something on her phone. "Hawg, I think Tightania is perfect for you. And, Romeo, I've got a new girl named Shantel whose mouth, I've heard, certainly knows how to make a man come."

Two girls arrived at the entrance. The brunette wore a black teddy and boasted an impressive rack. Not as big as Candy's, but a man could certainly fuck between them. She smiled and took Hawg's hand, leading him into the sinful delights of the back rooms.

"Hello," the other woman said. Romeo assumed she was Shantel. Her caramel skin gleamed in the low light, and his dick rose in anticipation of just how good her mouth had been advertised. She held out her hand, and he took it willingly, ready to lose himself for a few minutes in an orgasmic high.

Shantel led him to a room minimally decorated with only a bed, a table and a chair. But he supposed nothing more was needed. On the table lay an assortment of sex toys, a couple of bottles of lube and a plethora of condoms. *Nothing like being prepared.*

Although she was certainly beautiful, the wear and tear of Shantel's profession had begun to wreak havoc on her face and body. She looked tired. Emotionless. A calculating glimmer was the only thing in her dark eyes before she quickly lowered her gaze. Candy had promised a woman who knew how to get his rocks off with a very talented mouth, and he hoped she could deliver on that promise. Shantel fell to her knees, undoing his pants to pull them down far enough for his cock to emerge. Not even looking at him, she slurped his pre-cum up, one long, slow slide of her tongue from under the base to the slit. Her warm little tongue dipped into the hole, as if seeking more moisture, and he threaded his fingers in her hair to guide the blow job.

"Fuck, yeah," he panted. This was what he needed to relax the stress he'd been going through. It was one of the reasons why he liked coming to the Whiskey Lick Her. Good pussy was good pussy.

She lengthened how she pumped him with her mouth, allowing his cock to go farther, deeper, as her throat muscles relaxed.

"Touch my balls, baby," he ordered.

Obeying, she palmed his heavy sac and squeezed it, rolling the balls through the thin skin. Romeo gave a heavy gasp, thrusting his hips up into her mouth. Little by little, Shantel increased the tempo, speeding up.

"You gonna swallow me, baby?"

He took her moan as acquiescence and let go, shooting his cum down her throat. And being the talented whore she was, Shantel sucked him down, milking him for every drop he spewed out.

When it was over and his climax ebbed, all the shit the club was going through in his mind roared back twice as bad. Guilt for enjoying himself, even if only for ten or fifteen minutes, hit him hard, and he pushed Shantel away. The whore fell on her ass and she glared at him for a moment before pushing to her feet.

"You don't have to be so rough, asshole," she snapped. Before he could blink, she brought her fist back and punched him right in his nuts.

Unbelievable pain exploded through him, bringing tears to his eyes. His body caved in on itself and he dropped to his knees to cup his genitals protectively. Stars flashed behind his closed eyes. He could no longer hold back the moan of agony.

As he floundered for breath, he heard Shantel snicker at his misery. It took everything in him to push aside his suffering and rise to his feet. He shot out his hand and grabbed her chin, squeezing hard. She whimpered from the pain but he didn't give a fuck.

"You trying to fucking maim me, bitch?" He snarled the question.

Defiance poured out of her eyes.

"You can thank my sister-in-law I don't punch women." He yanked her so close their noses touched. "Not even cunts like you."

He pushed her, hard, and she fell back, banging into the nightstand and sending the lamp smashing onto the floor with a loud crash. Shantel looked at him through hate-filled eyes. It was only the fact that he refused to hit a woman that stayed his fist from striking her across the face.

"Get dressed," he ordered as he stepped back and pulled up his pants. "I don't fucking get you. The Men of Hell make sure you aren't smacked around, but, in return, your job is to pretend all the fucking you do is fan-fucking-tastic. How many other paying clients you hit in the nut sac?"

She didn't answer. She jerked her chin up in a mutinous tilt. In that instant, he saw that she truly hated either him or her life. Fine. If she didn't want his protection, he wouldn't force a woman to be a whore. He left the room, slamming the door behind him, and made his way to the front where Candy stood. She frowned at him and took a quick glimpse at her watch.

"Something wrong?"

Romeo nodded. "That bitch is gone, you hear me?"

"Shantel?"

"She's gone, Candy."

Not waiting for any other reply, he stormed out and headed to the bar. He needed a fucking drink. There were a shit load of things he should concentrate on, figure out, but hell if he wanted to do that right then. He was slowly transitioning into the club president, but for the next few hours, he was going to get lost in drink.

* * * *

Dax followed the car at a distance, but after the second turn, whoever was driving caught on that they were being followed. The expensive little car sped up, trying to lose him, but Dax was persistent. Down Cedar Road, onto Grant, until the driver managed to get onto the rural county road that led out of town. Dax shifted the bike into full throttle and easily caught up with the speeding car. He couldn't see inside, but he gestured to the driver to pull over. The Mercedes braked and fishtailed a little, but eventually it pulled to a stop. Dax rolled in front of the car and hit out his kickstand. Then he stomped over to the driver's window and knocked.

It took a moment for the driver to respond. The door opened and he waited, his hand loose and ready to grab his gun if he needed it. However, the first thing he saw was legs. Long, shapely legs, followed by a small waist, breasts and a gorgeous face frowning at him as she exited the car. The petite woman glared at him with eyes so dark they glowed with black fire. Horns stuck up on either side of her head and he blinked in confusion until he realized her hair was in some weird updo, emphasizing her Asian heritage. Interest stirred, and he tried hard to remember that she'd spent the better part of a week stalking the club.

"Who are you?" he demanded.

The delicate little chin went up a notch. "Shouldn't I be asking you that? You were chasing me for some reason."

He put his hands on his hips. "You deny you've been spying on us?"

"Yes." She crossed her arms, which thrust her tits out nicely. Her hip jutted to one side and he couldn't help but think she looked badass in her tight black jeans and high-heeled boots. And he tended to like badass chicks.

"Liar."

Anger darkened her features. "How dare you? You don't even know me!"

"You're right," he replied smoothly and walked around her to the open car door.

"What are you doing?" she demanded.

She punched his arm with her little fists, which amounted to a fly hitting him. *She's really cute when she's mad.* He sat in the driver's seat and adjusted it enough so he wasn't squished. A digital camera rested in the passenger side so he scooped it up.

"Hey!" she yelled.

She tried to grab the camera out of his hands, but he twisted his body to keep her away.

"That's private property. You have no right—"

"And you *are* a liar," he muttered as he scrolled through the photos. He was featured in some, all from standing in front of the Whiskey Lick Her. But the rest were of Romeo. Dozens of photos of his friend, captured in different poses, coming and going from the compound, sitting at the bar. "Who the *fuck* are you?"

She hurried around to the other side of the car and opened the door. She yanked the camera from his hand, and he let her have it back without a struggle. Then she slammed the door shut and stomped around to his side again, standing toe to toe with him even as he straightened to his six-foot-two height. She didn't cower, just stared up at him with a challenging scowl. The jut of her chin, the sneer in her lip, and the defiance in her eyes caused desire to punch his gut with a steel fist, and he didn't like it. Not one bit.

"I'm waiting," he said with a growl.

"None of your business," she replied coldly.

He grabbed her upper arms and spun her around until her back rested against the car door. He fitted his own body against hers, and, almost immediately, he realized his mistake as the hot outline of her pussy cradled his pelvis. His cock answered the call and hardened. Her eyes widened at his reaction. Their gazes met, held. Something wild and potent crashed into him going about the speed of a freight train. Her little pink tongue darted out to lick her lips and he had the craziest urge to kiss her until they both drowned in each other.

What the hell is wrong with me?

"Let me go," she said, but the anger had melted from her tone.

She seemed to feel the electric charge between them too. It wasn't just in his imagination. Her nipples beaded under her shirt, poking against him, and he couldn't help grinding his dick into the cradle of her thighs.

She gasped but didn't try to pull away. Instead, she studied him intently, like a bug under a microscope. He was hard pressed not to squirm from the examination.

"Not until you tell me your name and why you're here." The demands of his cock be damned.

"I'm Chloe," she answered softly.

Her pretty face now bore uncertainty, something he could relate to. He'd never had such a visceral reaction to a woman before, and it was utterly unnerving.

"Who are you spying for?"

She didn't answer, at least not right away. Instead, a myriad of emotions filtered through her almond-shaped eyes. There they stood, standing in the middle of the road under the bright moonlight, and Dax had the strangest notion to kiss her. The feeling only intensified when her gaze lingered on his mouth.

"Myself," she said softly.

"Uh... What?"

"I'm spying for myself."

He blinked. "Why?"

"Romeo Barrigan saved my cousin," she replied. "I moved to Bair in the hopes of repaying the debt."

"So you're what? Stalking him?"

"I call it learning."

She licked her lips, and he lost his train of thought. She managed to wiggle one hand free and lifted it to his face. He was a whole foot taller than she was, so she had to stretch, but she traced over his whiskered cheeks with featherlight touches. He didn't want to acknowledge just how much he enjoyed it.

"You're quite handsome," she murmured.

"You're quite beautiful."

She smiled at that. "What's your name?"

"Dax."

"You have to release me, Dax."

He nodded, not really comprehending what she'd said until her hands rested on his chest and pushed. He took a few steps back, although he didn't want to. His cock wanted right back between her thighs — preferably without clothes between them.

"Tell Romeo I said hello." Her gaze fell to his lips. "I think I'd like to run into you again, Daxton Squire."

She slipped into her car, started it, backed up a little then drove around his bike. Once again, he was staring at the tail lights. Only then did he realize that he'd never told her his full name.

Chapter Four

As soon as she entered her home, Chloe headed right to her laptop and turned it on. While she waited for it to boot up, she plugged her camera into the computer via a USB port and, minutes later, scrolled through all the photos she'd taken from her stakeout. When Dax's face lit up her screen, she halted. Confusion swirled within her. This wasn't how her tangents worked. She became fixated on one man, not two—just one. Yet, as she stared into his dark eyes, she couldn't deny the zing that shot through her body. Even in a photograph, he attracted her. Had something shifted? Had she lost her fixation?

She quickly clicked on Romeo's picture. She'd managed to capture him on his bike as he'd taken off his helmet. His T-shirt and cut stretched tightly over his muscles, outlining every detail. The distance prevented the camera from capturing his electric blue gaze, and as she zoomed in on his face, it simply pixilated even further. Still, she squirmed a little on the seat and her pussy clenched, yearning for a cock to fill it. His cock. Oh yes, she wanted him, but now she wanted Dax too.

What did that mean?

Confusion rolled through her. Since she still had feelings for Romeo, why had her body heated up when Dax had pressed up against her? The bristles of his beard had been soft under her touch, and she had very nearly kissed him. What would she do if given the opportunity to kiss Dax again? What if he was standing near Romeo when this so-called chance presented itself?

What if she was with *both* of them?

That was an interesting concept.

She printed out some of the better pictures of Romeo she had managed to capture, plus she impulsively printed the one of Dax, and brought them all over to her new collage. Since she had zero friends and family in Bair, she could put them blatantly on her bedroom walls without fear that someone would see them and think she was slipping again.

Her shrink would have had a field day if he could have seen her bedroom now. No doubt, he'd want to put her back on anti-depressants, make her leave Bair, get rid of all her triggers. He might even want to hospitalize her again. Fuck that. Her tangents didn't hurt people. In fact, it could be quite an enjoyable scenario for both parties if her infatuations would just stop saying that she was harassing them. The moment the cops were called was when her little fantasy world unraveled.

She readied herself for bed, trying her damnedest to forget about her reaction to Daxton Squire. After showering and brushing her teeth, she slipped naked between the covers. But lying in the dark didn't shut off her brain, and every second that passed, her pussy grew slicker. Butterflies swarmed through her belly until she couldn't resist the pull any longer. Reaching into the side table, she pulled out her vibrator and a picture of Romeo, only this time she added Dax's picture to the visual stimulation.

Chloe laid her six-inch masturbation friend aside before teasing her hard nipples. Her sexual appetite was great, hindered only by her little problem. It seemed like she couldn't find desire with any man other than the one she lusted for. Or, in this case, the *men*.

As she stared at Dax and Romeo, she teased her pussy lips apart and slipped two fingers into her extremely wet cunt and pumped them in and out a few times. She bit her lip as pleasurable quivers rattled through her then pulled them out to lick them clean.

She groped for the vibrator, eventually finding it in the sheets, and clicked it on. It pulsed in her hand noisily, so she turned it down to the medium setting before bringing it against one beaded nipple, rolling it over the peak. At the gentle vibrations against her soft skin, her clit pulsed with expectation. She returned the fingers she'd been sucking between her thighs, fucking her pussy as she pressed the vibrator directly on her nipple and flicked the setting to high.

A mini climax tore through her. She wasn't the type of girl who held back, because she could easily have multiple orgasms, but she wanted the big shebang as quickly as possible. Staring at two men, imagining all they could do to her, made her so hot and bothered she plunged the pink penis into her without any more preamble. Even wet, it took her a moment to get past the initial burn of invasion and to adjust by withdrawing and easing forward several times. Once she'd acclamated, she pumped the dildo in and out with one hand, and with the other, she massaged her clit vigorously.

"Oh, my God!" she cried out as she arched her back. She could only imagine Dax's mouth sucking on her tits while Romeo fucked her good and deep.

Her pussy made a squelching sound as the scent of her musky wetness filled her nostrils. She squirmed on the bed as pleasure flowed from where the long, thick toy vibrated inside her pussy. She soon fucked more strongly up against the toy and her fingers massaging her clit.

"Oh yes, fuck me hard," she called out to her imaginary lover. "Ram that cock deep." In her fantasy, he came inside her pussy, filling her up. Only now, there were two men, and just as Romeo slipped out of her, Dax would surge in, taking over. His huge dick would push out Romeo's cum, and it would run down the crack of her ass. One day, she would want them both to take her at the same time, one surging into her pussy while the other slid deep into her ass.

"Yes! Yes!" she whispered hoarsely as the peak hit her. Just the image of both men taking her had her coming so hard she saw stars.

When her body finally came down from its high, she became aware that she was sprawled naked on her bed. It highlighted that she was alone. While momentarily satisfying, her masturbation fantasy ultimately left her lonely. She turned off the pink dick and tossed it into her nightstand, deciding to wash it tomorrow. Her body had that nice relaxed feeling, but her soul remained empty. She wondered, as she always did, what it would take to fill it up.

And a small voice deep in her head questioned if someone as twisted as she was had the right to find happiness.

* * * *

The next morning, Romeo wandered down from the second floor, where his room was located, and into the large clubhouse kitchen. The smell of bacon and eggs turned his stomach and he walked to the bar and signaled to the prospect behind the counter to pour him a cup of black coffee.

"Rough night?" Hawg asked. "Didn't think the pussy was that bad."

"Don't want to talk about it," Romeo muttered as he sipped the strong brew. "Dax here?"

"Yeah, out in the garage."

Romeo nodded his thanks and headed through the clubhouse and out of the back door. Too-fucking-bright sunlight hit his eyes, sending daggers into his brain. He groaned and hurried into the garage. Dax was at his bike, tuning it up, and Romeo leaned over and grabbed the glasses off his nose.

"Hey," Dax protested.

"I'm using my presidential privilege to steal these," Romeo said as he settled them on his face. Instantly, the incessant glare of the sun eased.

Dax set down a wrench and smirked. "Hangover, eh?"

"Man, I am getting too old for drinking until I puke."

"And I *know* you're too old when you say shit like that. Should I call the nursing home now?"

Romeo flipped him off and drank more coffee from his mug. Dax picked up a rag and wiped off his hands.

"By the way, I met up with the person in that Mercedes," he said.

"Don't tell me it was the Shanks."

Dax shook his head. "Turns out you have a stalker."

The cup halted halfway to Romeo's mouth. "Come again?"

"Her name is Chloe," Dax said. He sat on his bike and crossed his arms. "Said you saved her cousin and now wants to repay the debt."

Romeo's brain hurt too much to think. "*Did* I save her cousin?"

Dax shrugged. "I don't know *that*, but I do know she's a hot piece of ass that has the hots for you."

Romeo stared at his best friend, unsure if he was trying to fuck with him or not. They'd both grown up in the MC, although Dax had been there a whole year before he had shown up. Romeo's father had been a nomad, a drifter going from club to club, and his mother was a club whore. The last thing either had wanted was a kid tying them down. After playing house for so many years, they'd left him with Wheels, giving him a shove on the shoulder and a nonchalant wave of goodbye. In the beginning, Dax loved to taunt, tease and torment him at every opportunity, and sometimes Dax fell back into his juvenile stupidity.

"How hot are we talking?" he asked skeptically. Okay, so maybe he did too.

"She's got an ass I'd love to bite," Dax admitted.

"Hmm. How do you know she's a stalker?"

"Dude, I scrolled through the pictures on her camera." Dax scrunched up his nose. "Dozens of you. I wasn't able to determine if she was a threat to you or not, but I plan on hunting her down to find out."

"You think she might be part of those men questioning Creole Jack?"

Dax frowned. "Anything is possible, and I certainly don't trust her as far as I can throw her. For now, don't go anywhere alone."

"Oh, for fuck's sake," Romeo muttered. He really didn't need one more thing added to his plate. "I'm not a baby, Dax."

"And it's my job to protect you," Dax said sternly. "I've done a shitty job for this club so far, so just do as I fucking say. All right?"

"You haven't done a shitty job, Dax."

Dax just shrugged. "Something is happening, or going to happen. I can feel it. And until we know exactly what it is, I don't trust the girl with a camera, Drifter, Bandit, the Shanks, or you riding alone. Got it?"

Romeo held up his hands in a surrender gesture. "Got it."

"Romeo!"

Romeo's name boomed within the compound, and he looked out of the garage bay to see his VP waving at him near the gate. He set his coffee cup on the tool chest and hurried toward Boone. Dax followed. The compound's gate had been rolled back and two large coolers pulled inside.

"What's this?"

"Hook rolled up to the gate and saw these coolers resting in front," Boone said.

"Anyone see who brought them?"

A round of "No" came from the assembled men. Romeo went to open one, but Dax placed a hand on his arm and shook his head.

"No. Let me."

Romeo took a step back, frowning. "You think it could be rigged with explosives?"

"I don't know," Dax said. "My gut feeling, remember? There's too many situations developing and I don't like it."

"Well, I'm not going to stand by while you get blown to smithereens either," Romeo replied. "Find a way to open it from a distance."

For clever men, Romeo pursed his lips as he surveyed their bright idea of opening the coolers. It consisted of them hiding behind a truck and using a long metal rod to pop the lid. When nothing went ka-boom, he rolled his eyes and marched past all the 'fraidy cats and peered into the coolers.

The lifeless eyes of Babyface stared up at him. His severed head lay on top of his torso. Romeo opened the second cooler and found the rest of him. A note had been placed between his fingers.

"Holy shit," Dax muttered.

"Fuck," Boone swore.

The rest of the Brothers gathered around. One turned away to vomit. They were all hardened men, seasoned to hurt—or kill—if they had to. But it took a certain level of depravity to cut up a person and stuff the parts into coolers. Romeo's hungover stomach rolled at the sight of the prospect chopped up like fish bait.

"I asked him to follow you last night, make sure you got back to the compound okay," Romeo whispered. Tears pricked his eyes.

"I didn't..." Dax's voice cracked and he cleared his throat. "I didn't come straight here."

The implication was clear and Romeo glanced at him. "Someone was waiting at the club. This could've been you."

"No, Rome," Dax said, shaking his head. "This was meant to be *you*."

Rattled, Romeo took the note that Babyface clutched then closed the lid on both coolers. The prospect had only been twenty, nicknamed Babyface because he couldn't even grow a proper beard. Now he lay in pieces, delivered like fucking mail.

He unfolded the note. "The Men of Hell will be dismantled piece by piece unless you leave Bair immediately."

"What the fuck?" Boone growled and snatched the note out of Romeo's hand to read it for himself. "Is this a fucking joke?"

Gabby took the piece of paper from him and held it up to the light. But, as usual, he didn't comment on why he was doing that.

"I want to know who the fuck did this," Romeo said coldly, pointing to the coolers. Fury washed through him, leaving a wake of freezing ice behind. It fueled him. "If it was the Shanks, I want to destroy them. If it was someone else, I want them hunted down and their fucking heads on pikes. Understood?"

Every member nodded grimly.

"Make sure Babyface gets a decent burial," he added. "He has a mother out in Red Vine. I'll ride and tell her."

Boone clasped his hand on Romeo's shoulder. "Gabby and I will go with you."

"I'll take care of the body," Dax added.

Romeo nodded, too choked up to say anything else. He placed his hand on the closed cooler once more before marching away. What the hell was going on? *Who cuts a man into pieces and gives him back to his family stuffed into coolers?*

He stormed into his office and slammed the door shut. He craved privacy, but, almost immediately, the four walls closed in on him. The patch on his cut proclaiming him president was like a noose, cinching a little tighter every day. He'd never wanted the damn thing, even though Wheels had practically trained him to replace him one day. When Shepard had decided to take over, Romeo had secretly been relieved. And now this was his fault. What had happened to Babyface rested squarely on his shoulders because he hadn't acted like a proper president and had neglected to lock down all the things that needed to be figured out. With a roar, he swiped off everything from his desktop, smashing it all on the floor.

Just like the chair, this stuff was tainted too.

He grabbed the fire extinguisher sitting in the corner, the one that had about an inch of dust on it, and began hitting the desk. Again and again, he bashed in the old, tough wood that had served the Men of Hell president faithfully for forty years. The blows reverberated through the metal canister and up into his arms, but he welcomed the pain. His avoidance had almost brought about the ruin of the club, and if he didn't grow some steel balls and become a fucking leader, then Babyface's death wouldn't be avenged. Hell, he could fight, maim and kill all night long, but figuring things out and trying to think two steps ahead was something he'd never counted on doing. One thing a president did was keep his men safe—and he'd failed.

Someone knocked sharply upon the door.

"Come in," he barked. Sweat rolled off him from the exertion of destroying the desk.

Dax poked his head inside. "You finished breaking everything?"

Romeo tossed the fire extinguisher onto the pile of broken wood. It clanked loudly and rolled, making even more clangs and clashes. "Yep."

"Feel any better?"

"Nope."

"Okay. I was wondering if you had a moment."

Romeo placed his hands on his hips and gestured to one of the chairs that had been pushed back during his rampage. When Dax sat down, Romeo dropped into the other one and stared at the pile of rubble between them.

"I have Frank from the funeral home coming to pick Babyface up," Dax said. "He'll do him right."

"Yeah," Romeo muttered. "Frank is a good guy."

"At some point I want to find Chloe and question her."

"You think she's involved with what happened to Babyface?"

"I don't know, but it can't be coincidence that she's in town and shit starts happening."

Romeo shrugged. "Sure. Have fun torturing her."

"Afterward, I thought I would go track down Mendoza and shake information out of him. If he and his men have any, that is. I'm not too sure this was their work, though. Not their MO."

"We can't rule anyone out." Romeo looked around at the destruction of his office. "I'll meet up with you after I talk with Babyface's mom so we can question Mendoza together."

Dax shook his head. "No."

"They threatened the club, not me."

"You *are* the club, Rome. What d'ya think will happen if you get gunned down? This club has been through too much. It'll implode."

Romeo sighed and ran a hand through his hair. "I hear what you're saying, but I'm pulling rank, Daxton Christopher Squire."

"Shit. I *hate* it when you use my middle name."

Romeo smiled, although he didn't feel any amusement. All that consumed him was vengeance. The need to hurt the ones who had killed Babyface burned through his soul, and he was more than happy to embrace the flames.

Chapter Five

Red Vine was located in the middle of nowhere and boasted a convenience store that also doubled for a gas station and a place to buy groceries. The population sign stated that it had about four hundred people, but fuck if Romeo knew where those people were hiding.

Babyface's mom lived in a mobile home that had rooms built onto it, no doubt, to make it bigger. The mishmash of materials used, however, only emphasized the poverty. Well, that and the numerous vehicles in the yard sitting on cinder blocks, rusting away little by little.

He, Boone and Gabby pulled to a stop near the end of the gravel driveway and turned off their bikes. A large woman carrying a shotgun marched out of the front door. She wore a muumuu and a cigarette dangled from her mouth. From the side of the house stepped a middle-aged man with greasy hair and a paunch belly, wiping his hands on his dirty overalls. A gun belt hung around his hips.

"Mrs. Stillwater?"

"Who wants to know?" the old woman asked.

"My name is Romeo. This is Boone and Gabby. We're with the Men of Hell."

"Yeah, I can see that." The shotgun lowered a fraction. "You're here to tell me bad news about my boy, ain't you?"

Romeo nodded.

"He was kilt?" the man asked.

"Yes, sir," Boone replied softly.

Mrs. Stillwater looked away for a moment. The shotgun hung limp in her hand. "I don't have any money if you're looking for help to bury him."

"The club is going to give him a proper burial," Boone replied softly. "He wasn't a full member yet, but he was a good man. A loyal prospect."

Mrs. Stillwater nodded sadly. "He was my only boy. Got me a couple of girls who don't care about their mama, but Joshua came by regularly to make sure I was okay."

"Do you know who did it?" the man asked. "I'm his...was...his uncle."

Romeo shook his head. "Not yet."

The man reached up and took hold of his sister's hand. "What'll you do when you do find out?"

"I plan to tear him to fucking pieces," Romeo promised solemnly.

"Good," Mrs. Stillwater said. "You do that for my boy." Grief hunched her shoulders, her face a mask of misery and regret. Just as a tear escaped from her eye, she spun away and headed back into the trailer.

"We're so sorry," Romeo told Babyface's uncle, then he turned to get back on his bike. Anger churned in his gut. There was no way he was going to reveal to Mrs. Stillwater just how her son had died, how he'd been disrespected. "We should be able to compensate her."

"With what money?" Boone asked as he straddled his bike.

"I don't know. And I know money can't possibly make up for losing a kid, but I want to help her."

Boone glanced at Gabby. "Listen, I have a bit of cash saved up. We can send that to Mrs. Stillwater if you want."

Romeo frowned. "I wouldn't ever ask you to do something like that. You earned that money."

Boone shrugged. "It's yours if you want it."

"Thanks," Romeo said. "Boone, do you...?"

"Do I what?" Boone prompted.

"Do you think Wheels made a mistake about me?"

Boone stared at him with his cool gray eyes. Behind him, Gabby stared at him too. Romeo met their scrutiny without fidgeting under their intense appraisals.

"This club is at a crossroads," Boone finally said. "And I think Wheels saw this coming years ago. Now you have a choice. You can be the man who got the name Romeo by burying himself in pussy, or you can be the president Wheels always thought you could be. But you can't waver and you can't ignore what this club needs."

It wasn't until they were halfway back to the compound that Romeo realized Boone had never answered his question.

* * * *

Monday came all too soon and this time Chloe was stuck doing urology procedures. One thing she'd learned long ago in this job was that seventy-year-old cocks were vastly different from thirty-year-old cocks. Pulling kidney stones out of shriveled urethras wasn't her favorite task at all.

So when lunchtime rolled around, she wasn't in the best of moods and sneered when she walked into the break room. Someone with seriously bad taste in rustic country charm had gotten their hands on decorations for the area. Cutesy wooden cutouts of farm animals, adorned with calico material, took up every available space. Even the table and chairs were nightmares from a craft store hell, with cow seat cushions and salt and pepper shakers shaped like pigs. The urge to vomit every time she walked into it cramped Chloe's stomach.

Susan, the snob OR nurse—as Chloe liked to think of her—sat perched on the edge of her chair as she blew on a steaming cup of tea. She was so not the person Chloe wanted to deal with, but short of denying herself lunch, she couldn't kick the woman out.

"So how was your weekend?" Susan asked brightly.

"Fine."

"I can't imagine what you did, stuck here."

Chloe shrugged. She didn't want to answer and encourage more idle chitchat.

Susan didn't pick up on the mental thought. Nor, did it seem, was she prone to mind control. "Then again, I don't know what possessed you to move to Bair in the first place."

Chloe popped the lid on her soda.

"There is absolutely nothing here except dirty bikers and dirty gang bangers," Susan continued. "Of course, those bastards are what keeps this job interesting. It's a shame that the cops can't just go in, drop a few bombs into their little club and put us all out of our misery. I bet if those ugly bikers went away, the drug gang would go away too. You know how awful those types of people are."

Anger surged through Chloe, but she bit her bottom lip to help defuse her instinct to do something impulsive. Just because Susan rubbed her the wrong way wasn't reason enough to punch her.

"So why did you move here?" Susan asked again. One corner of her mouth curled upward and her eyes narrowed speculatively. "Are you crazy or something? Is that why you moved to shithole Bair, Nebraska? Only someone escaping the loony bin would move here willingly."

Out of everything Susan could've said, she'd had to use the word crazy. It was a taunt Chloe couldn't ignore. She could handle a confusing weekend and a shitty morning, but what she couldn't cope with was her sanity being called into question. She *wasn't* crazy until someone pointed out that maybe she was.

Chloe walked over to the chair and kicked it out from under Susan's ass. The nurse went down, chin first, which hit the surface of the table. She let out a cry of pain as blood gushed from her mouth. No doubt, the bitch had bitten through her viperous tongue.

Chloe leaned over her. "You say one more derogatory remark against me or the Men of Hell and more than your tongue will need stitches," she said softly. "From now on, you'll only say nice things about us, or nothing at all. Do you understand me, Susan?"

Susan stared at her in pure terror through wide, pain-glazed eyes. Tears ran down the woman's cheeks, but Chloe was immune to the sympathy they should've invoked. She had no pity for people who pissed her off. When Susan nodded jerkily, Chloe smiled and eased back.

"Excellent," she replied. "You asked if I was crazy and I hope I answered your question. Don't forget that I know where you live, Susan, so let's keep this between us besties, all right?"

Again, Susan nodded, terror and pain mixing equally on her face.

Chloe raised her voice. "We need some help in here!"

A second later, a doctor rushed into the room. "Oh, my God! What happened?"

"She just slipped," Chloe said, schooling her features into a mask of concern. "I opened my soda, took a drink, and heard her hit the table. It was awful."

"Aw, Susan," the doctor said. "I think you're going to need stitches. Come with me."

The doctor slipped his arm around Susan's shoulders to help her out of the break room. Chloe couldn't help but wink at her as she passed.

* * * *

After the fervor of Susan's 'accident' had died down, the rest of the work day blew by quickly and Chloe's last case of the day was a tractor accident where a man had impaled himself. Once the spike had been removed, they'd had to do an exploratory surgery to make sure no internal organs had been damaged. She'd put in an hour of overtime and was one of the last people to leave for the day. As she exited the hospital, she saw Dax sitting on the hood of her Mercedes. His bike rested benignly beside her car.

The little thrill of excitement that shot through her confused the hell out of her since she'd half convinced herself that her response to Daxton Squire had been a figment of her imagination. There was no explanation for how her nipples turned into aching pebbles of excitement or how her pussy slicked the closer she walked toward him.

"How long have you been here?" she asked as she unlocked the car doors and tossed in her purse.

"Long enough to wave at all your co-workers."

"Hmm," she said. "How'd you find me?"

"Your car kind of stands out."

She pursed her lips as she looked over the black Mercedes. "I suppose it does. This car wasn't my choice. My grandfather insisted when I graduated."

Dax whistled. "Nice grandfather. Should I volunteer to be your boy toy? I wouldn't mind a new Harley SuperLow."

"Why do I get the feeling you're not here for light sexual banter?"

He rose from the hood of her car and crossed his arms as he studied her. She couldn't help thinking he was measuring her up for some reason.

"One of my club Brothers was killed Saturday night," he said.

Panic flooded through her. She stepped up to Dax and placed her hands upon his folded arms. "Is Romeo okay?"

He cocked his head. "Romeo is pissed off, but fine."

Relief crashed through her, leaving her a little dizzy and a little guilty. A club Brother had lost his life but all she cared about was that it wasn't her man. "Who?"

"Babyface. He was a prospect."

"I'm sorry, Dax. What happened?"

"He was murdered."

"Shanks?"

"How do you know about the Shanks?" he demanded.

She crossed her arms and raised an eyebrow. "Really? You think I wouldn't know about Romeo's enemies?"

"Up until this moment, I half wondered if you were involved."

"What?" she gasped. "I would never hurt Romeo, or the club."

"I don't know anything about you, Chloe, except you're a stalker. Why *wouldn't* I suspect you?"

She was getting a little tired of people labeling her as obsessive, crazy and a stalker. Hadn't Dax listened to *anything* she'd said last night? "I told you, I'm here to repay a debt."

"Yeah, one Romeo doesn't even remember."

She frowned. "He doesn't remember? But... He was so kind."

"Kind? Are you sure you have the right Romeo?"

"Of course, Dax." She waved her hand. "It doesn't matter if he remembers. I still owe him. But if it wasn't the Shanks, then who was it?"

Dax didn't say anything. He just stood staring at her—measuring her. Her heart sped up as their eyes met, locked. His brown eyes weren't as dark as hers—milk chocolate to her near obsidian. He searched the depths of her soul. She wasn't sure what he was looking for, but she hoped he figured out she wasn't here to hurt Romeo. Finally, he sighed and rubbed the back of his neck, glancing away from her.

"We're going to have a little meeting with their leader later tonight, but I don't think it's them. This killing was...brutal. Precise. The Shanks are more killers of opportunity."

"Is Romeo in danger?" she asked. She had to know. If he was, it changed everything.

"There was a message sent, telling us to get out of Bair or we'd all be taken apart piece by piece."

A chill swept through her. Someone was threatening her man. Or…men?

"Why are you here, Chloe?"

"I told you why I came here."

"For Romeo?"

"Yes."

He nodded, as if he'd expected that answer. "Stop following him. Whoever killed our prospect targeted us, waited for him. It was an ambush. I don't want you to be in the wrong place at the wrong time."

She lifted her chin. "I can take care of myself."

He took a step closer, crowding her. He tried to intimidate her with his size, but all it caused was a thrilling shot of lust to wash through her. "Listen, Chloe, this isn't a fucking game. Babyface came back to us in pieces. You should go home, little girl. Go back to the money you seem to have grown up in."

He left her standing there, marched toward his motorcycle and put his helmet on. He straddled his bike then looked at her. Once again, their gazes met. Held. For a moment, heat flashed through his dark orbs. He stared at her hungrily and an answering call rose in her blood. Then he started his bike and took off with a roar of its powerful engine. She watched after him until he was long gone, and still she hesitated in the near empty parking lot.

She'd known Romeo would need her, and this time it was real, not just an obsessive love-induced hallucination. Chloe unlocked her car and slid behind the wheel. The engine purred to life, and during the whole ride back to her apartment, she couldn't help comparing Romeo with Nathan. She hadn't met the leader of the Men of Hell—at least not yet—but already she knew Romeo was completely different from the doctor with whom she'd had a previous tangent episode. It was over Nathan that doctors had bandied about the word obsessive and co-workers had whispered 'crazy' behind their hands. She'd lost her job, her self-respect, and it had brought her grandfather back into her life.

For a while, she'd even believed them. She'd taken their drugs and had stayed in a posh resort while she recuperated from her mental break, wondering all the while why someone hadn't done this when she was thirteen. Shouldn't a child who'd been abused by her mother need the same tiptoeing care? No one had figured it out then, just as no one understood now, and on the heels of that realization, Chloe had checked herself out and chucked her meds down the toilet.

Shaking the memories away was the only way she could cope. Once inside her apartment, she set her purse down and hurried into her bedroom to pull out the file on the club she'd taken from her grandfather's office. She read the assembled data until she arrived at the information on the drug gang operating in the small town. The Shanks didn't seem very well organized, mostly relying on brute strength and threats as they peddled their prescription drug trade. They dabbled in meth and pot, but they were noted mostly for trafficking Oxycontin and Vicodin along Interstate 80. The trade route was one reason why the Shanks and the Men of Hell didn't get along. Bair sat in a prime location, equidistant between Denver and Omaha.

Dax said they were going to hunt in the Shanks' end of town, so she laid out a street map and looked over where that was exactly. At first glance, Bair didn't seem all that big. The newer section was divided by the interstate, with the Men of Hell's compound about two miles south. Their bar, the Whiskey Lick Her, lay on that stretch of road. That long drive was nothing but farmland. On the northbound side of the interstate lay the rest of the town. Just past the obligatory gas station, McDonald's and crappy motel were the majority of small businesses and homes, including the hospital she worked in. She guessed it made sense for the pill pushers to be firmly settled into that area. The report stated their leader, a man named Mendoza, ran the junkyard just outside the town limits.

What if this Mendoza lay in wait for Romeo? What if there was an ambush, gun sights aimed directly on the MOH as they roared into their area? Harley's weren't exactly known for their stealth-like engines.

Dread settled in the pit of her stomach, gnawing at her insides like a carnivorous beast. What if Romeo was shot? What if he died? She had to do something. He *needed* her. Her gaze landed on her medical bag at the bottom of her closet. No doubt she'd be arrested for half the stuff she had in there, but it wasn't as if she'd stolen the medicine to make a little extra cash. She'd put it together for this very purpose.

Mind made up, she quickly changed out of her after-work clothes and hurried into her closet. She chose black stretch jeans, a black T-shirt and low-heeled boots for the night, before pulling her hair back into a ponytail. From a box under her bed, she pulled out her gun, a SIG Sauer Mosquito with a threaded barrel. She popped in a magazine and chambered a round before screwing on the sound suppressor. She flipped on the safety and laid it on the bed while she buckled on her custom-made gun belt, then she slipped the weapon into it. It rested on the small of her back, too bulky to be comfortable, but its presence was nonetheless soothing. She pocketed another full magazine, grabbed her medical bag then headed out the door.

Chapter Six

Great hulking wrecks of twisted metal and rusting car shells rose up in the moonlight as monolithic sculptures. Romeo, Dax, Boone and Gabby drove up to the fenced gate that should've been closed and locked at this hour, but stood wide open in a blatant invitation.

"This is a trap," Dax muttered, pissed off that he couldn't keep his president from leaving the safe confines of the compound. How could he do his job when the head honcho didn't heed him?

"I know," Romeo said. He flipped out his kickstand with his foot and rose from his bike. He yanked off his helmet and set it on the seat. The other men followed his lead.

"Stay here," Dax ordered Romeo.

Romeo gave him an incredulous look. "You fucking kidding me?"

"This is colossally dumb of us walking into Mendoza's territory." Dax pulled his gun from its holster. "You can bet he's looking at his video monitor saying hello stupid fuckers, come right on in and *die*."

"Gabby said quit your whining," Boone said.

Both Dax and Romeo frowned at Gabby. They hadn't heard a word from the big man.

As soon as they crossed into the junkyard, a smattering of bullets pinged all around them, bouncing off various objects. Thumps on the ground where other shots hit the dirt were like fragments of meteors. Sounds of weapon fire and the whizzing of the deadly orbs came too close to their heads. The acrid scent of old grease, rust and gunpowder permeated the air. Everything seemed to happen at once. Romeo cursed and ran. He and Dax headed one way while Gabby and Boone dashed to another route. The junkyard became a maze, and the bright moon wasn't helping them hide.

"God damn it!" Romeo growled. "They have the high ground."

"Yeah, well, this is *their* fucking place," Dax replied sarcastically.

They dove behind a crane, and Dax stuck his head out to survey the area. A body popped up along one of the ridgelines and he took aim and fired. The man grunted and fell back. One down, but how many more to go?

"We just want to talk, Mendoza!" Romeo shouted.

Shadows moved and a flow of bullets punched the area above Romeo's head, showering him with debris.

"Shit!" Dax cried and grabbed his friend to fling him to the ground. "Guess Mendoza doesn't want to talk."

"Yeah," Romeo said. "Ah, Christ, that hurts."

Dax reared back and stared in horror at the wet stain that grew on Romeo's upper arm. It had missed his cut by a sliver.

"Fuck, you're bleeding."

"No shit," Romeo muttered.

Dax tried to press his hand to the wound, but Romeo just knocked it away.

"Doesn't matter. Just a minor wound. We need to find Mendoza."

A splattering of shots fired again, and Dax clamped a hand on Romeo's good arm to drag him over to a pile of flattened cars.

Dax ducked his head around the corner of the heap of metal. "I can't see Boone or Gabby. We need to get you to the hospital."

"Fuck the hospital. I need to make sure the Shanks didn't kill Babyface."

"You can't question anyone if you're dead," Dax said harshly.

"I'm fine, Dax."

"Of course you're not fine! You're fucking shot!"

A series of sounds echoed through the junkyard. *Pop! Pop, pop, pop.* Silence.

Dax cautiously peered around the car again. "What the fuck?"

"What is it?" Romeo asked. He then looked too.

Dax stared in disbelief at Chloe as she calmly walked toward them, dressed like she came from *The Expendables*, all in black with her ponytail swinging back and forth in time to her steady gait. In one hand, she clutched a gun with a silencer as she cautiously looked around. In the other hand, she held a black canvas bag.

"Why the hell is she here?" Dax wondered.

"Who is she?"

"That's Chloe."

"My stalker?" Romeo grinned. "I think I'm in love."

Dax threw him an exasperated look. He didn't have time for this right now. He quickly suppressed the jealousy that surged through him at Romeo's statement. He had no reason to feel anything but annoyance and anger that she'd disobeyed his command.

Chloe spotted him and sashayed her cute little ass over to them, as if she were taking a night-time stroll through a park. As soon as she was close enough, he grasped her arm and yanked her behind the car tower.

"Ow! What the hell, Dax?"

"There are men shooting," he snarled. "Did you not listen to a word I said?"

"I took care of those men," she said calmly as she removed herself from his tight grip.

"What do you mean you—?"

"Romeo, you're hit!" she cried. She scrambled over to him to survey the bullet in his arm. "It's still in there."

"I know," Romeo said through tight lips. Pain bracketed every line on his face. "Hi, I'm Romeo Barrigan. Nice to meet you. I hear you're my stalker."

She threw Dax the same kind of exasperated look he'd given Romeo. "I'm Chloe Matsumoto." From the depths of the bag she carried, she produced some gauze. Stamped in red across the package was the word 'sterile'. She pulled apart the edges and removed the pad inside. Romeo winced as she applied pressure to his wound. "I'm going to take care of you, okay?"

"In a chop-my-legs-off maniacal way or in a medical capacity?" he asked warily.

"Right now in a medical way, but we'll see how it goes," she replied, winking.

Dax wanted to gag. Seriously, was she flirting right now?

Romeo blinked and smiled. "Great."

Dax rolled his eyes.

"How did you find us?" Dax asked. He kept his tone angry to let her know he wasn't very thrilled at seeing her.

"You said you were going to question the leader of the Shanks," she answered softly, still focused on Romeo's wound. "I knew the leader, Mendoza, operated from the junkyard. It wasn't that hard to figure out."

"It's like pulling teeth with you," he muttered. "Every question you answer has new ones popping up. How'd you know about the junkyard?"

At that moment, Boone and Gabby suddenly appeared behind her. Gabby held a moaning man in his hands. Blood dripped from his obviously shattered kneecap.

"Someone shot the fuckers," Boone said. His gaze flickered questioningly over Chloe. "This one is still alive, so he should do well for interrogation. Who's she?"

"I'm Chloe," she said, smiling brightly. "I'm a friend."

Dax turned wide eyes on her. "Wait. *You* shot them?"

She shrugged. "I can shoot the wings off a fly if you want me to, but before we get into that pissing competition, help me get Romeo back to my car. I'll follow you to the clubhouse and treat him there."

"You're a nurse?" Boone asked.

"As close as you're gonna get right now," she replied. From her bag, she withdrew a small vial of clear liquid and a packaged sterile syringe.

"What's that?" Dax demanded.

"Just a very small dose of morphine to help manage the pain." She opened the syringe then filled it with the medicine and injected it into Romeo's biceps.

Almost immediately, his face relaxed as the pain presumably melted away.

"Oh, yeah," he murmured happily. "I really like morphine. I love you, Chloe."

She kissed his cheek and he grinned widely at her.

"Okay, enough," Dax growled.

Chloe dispensed with the used syringe into a small red container. "Let's get him back to the clubhouse. I don't want him to bleed to death in this fucking crap yard of junk."

As Boone helped Romeo to his feet, Chloe met Dax's gaze. Her eyes were haunting, her lips plump. Sure, she was gorgeous, but that wasn't what captivated him. Something sparked between them, sucker punching him in his gut and knocking all the air out of his lungs. He swore the earth tilted a little, just enough for his equilibrium to shift. He didn't know what the hell was happening, but when she turned away to hurry after Romeo, all he wanted to do was punch something.

Never in all his life had he ever been jealous of Romeo—until now. It clawed at his gut that she was here for him. That she only had her eyes set on him. That she was *Romeo's* fucking stalker.

Dax helped Romeo out of the junkyard and to her car while she and Boone held point, making sure they weren't ambushed again. Gabby brought up the rear, pulling the injured Shanks member along. They didn't have Mendoza, but they had one of his men, which was hopefully good enough to find out the information they needed.

"He can ride in my trunk," she said, nodding to the still bleeding, still moaning man. She popped the car's trunk and Gabby unceremoniously shoved the prisoner inside before shutting it with a firm click. "Romeo, you can ride with me—"

"No," he said immediately. "I need to ride my bike back."

"You can't ride with a busted shoulder."

"And I'm not leaving my bike here," he argued back. "I'll be fine."

She glanced at the other three, but Dax knew better than to correct Romeo and not just because he was their president. No member left a bike behind.

"Your shoulder—"

"I don't feel a thing."

"Yes, because I just gave you a shot of morphine," she argued. "You could crash."

"One little shot of morphine isn't going to make me crash," he said, placating. "I've been on worse highs, believe me. Just wrap up my shoulder enough for me to make it back."

Chloe huffed and puffed, clearly not liking this idea at all, but she opened her bag and pulled out some supplies. Dax helped Romeo take off his cut, then she wrapped an Ace bandage around the upper part of his arm. Minutes later, a huge pressure bandage soaked up any blood still leaking.

Romeo nodded his thanks and walked over to his bike. Dax was about to head toward his, but Chloe yanked Romeo's cut out of his hands.

"I'll take this," she said.

"I warned you to stay away," he admonished. "You didn't do as I said."

"I rarely do as I'm told."

"Yeah, I'm discovering that about you."

She stepped up to him until he felt her body heat enveloping him. There it was again, that spark that drove him batty. She may have the hots for Romeo, but there was no denying that chemistry flared between them. Suddenly he was more than willing to make her admit that her pussy creamed for him as well.

"I'll see you at the compound," she whispered.

"Definitely." He lowered his voice to the tone more than one woman had described as sexy. "We need to talk about your listening *skills*."

He made sure to put emphasis on the last word, lacing the statement with unspoken passionate promise. Her eyes widened a little and small gasp escaped her.

He turned, grinning. Making her concede to him would be so much fun.

Chapter Seven

Romeo cursed to himself as he rode back to the Men of Hell compound. Shit, the morphine had taken away the pain, but the drug was causing havoc to his eyesight. The fucking world shifted and changed while he stayed still, only he knew that wasn't right because he was on a motorcycle. Newton's laws of motion made sure he was still moving.

Maybe the chick was right. Chloe. Maybe he should've ridden with her, but he didn't trust his bike left in front of a junkyard, even if the owner was MIA. He'd worked hard to get his bike just how he wanted it and he'd be damned if he'd let a little bullet give it as a Christmas present to the Shanks.

He had to admit that if he was destined to have a stalker, he certainly was happy she was beautiful. And it was helpful that she knew her way around a bullet wound. Perhaps he could keep her for a little while, until her obsession with him dwindled. What harm was there if she was devoted to him?

When he finally turned into the open gate of the Men of Hell compound, relief gripped him. Sweat poured out of him and his hands shook with the exertion of not laying his bike down. He managed to flip out his kickstand and turn off his engine, but that was the moment his strength fled.

Dax hurried over to him and helped him off the bike. Romeo's knees wiggled like jelly, causing him to lean completely against his friend. Boone hurried over to help Dax guide him into the clubhouse, and by then, all the other members had run forward to clear a path on the couch so he could lie down. A few of the club girls leaned over him, clucking like mother hens.

"Oh, you poor thing!"

"Please don't die, Romeo!"

Chloe bustled over and shooed the women away with a death glare. "Get back. Get all the way back. In fact, never touch him again."

"Bitch," one mumbled.

"Say that to my face one more time and I'll break your fucking nose," Chloe said coldly. Deadly.

She may be a tiny thing, but Romeo saw a fierceness in her that made his dick sit up and salivate.

The girls must have seen it too. They backed down.

"You should go to the hospital," Dax told him again.

"I can take care of him," Chloe said, kneeling next to him with a bottle of iodine in her hand. "Are you allergic to iodine?"

"Not that I'm aware of," Romeo replied.

Dax laid a hand on her arm. "Wait. Do you know how to dig out a bullet from muscle?"

She nodded. "I assisted in a lot of shooting surgeries when I worked in LA. Luckily, this one didn't nick any of his bones or the brachial artery. Otherwise he *would* have to go the hospital."

"Just get the fucking thing out of my arm," Romeo muttered. "Dax, get that piece of Shanks shit strung up. I'll be out in a few minutes."

"You won't be able to move this arm," she said. "Definitely won't be able to torture anyone."

"That's why I have him," he replied with a nod toward Dax. "My own minion of evil."

Dax snorted. "You're fucking hilarious."

"Go, minion, do my bidding."

He smiled when he heard Dax's exasperated growl. He did that a lot around Romeo. He cracked open his eyes. Dax stared hungrily at Chloe. Even as horny teenagers sharing club pussy, he'd never seen Dax with such a look of longing. It made him wonder what lay between Chloe's legs that had the tough man so tangled up — and if his friend had already sampled the delectable treat.

A moment later, Dax turned and walked out of the clubhouse. Chloe watched him until the door closed, then she returned her attention to his wound. She gave him a series of shots until his arm went nicely numb. Then she swathed the area in a yellowish substance before putting on some sterile gloves. There was tugging but not any sharp pain, and his mind wandered while she took care of him. Her black hair gleamed in the overhead light, the midnight undertones almost blue. Of course, that could be the drug making him hallucinate. Still, he had the strangest urge to run his fingers through it.

"Are you?" Romeo asked softly.

"Am I what?"

"A stalker."

She shrugged, not looking at him. "I owe you, simple as that. A certain person seems to have taken exception to me learning your habits."

Her gaze flicked briefly over to the door through which Dax had exited. Something dark and telling shifted in her eyes before disappearing under her poker expression.

"Yeah, Dax mentioned that," he said. "I'm sorry, but I don't remember helping anyone."

She licked her lips. He couldn't seem to take his eyes off her glistening mouth and all sorts of filthy images filled his head. She'd look fucking gorgeous on her knees while she sucked his dick.

"Last year my cousin, Kaiya, was traveling to a symposium for the deaf," she said. "She was taken at night from outside her hotel."

A light bulb clicked on in his brain. He'd helped his brother Branch, his riding partner Charlie, and their old lady, Lily, capture the guy trafficking women. That prick had been the club's old president, Shepard.

"Wait," he said. "You're talking about the Master's house, in Missouri."

She nodded. A second later, the smashed, red-tinted bullet thudded harmlessly onto the floor.

"I remember her now," he mused. The mental picture of a beautiful Asian girl came easily from his memories. "I cut the ties off her wrists. What was her name again?"

"Kaiya."

"That's right. She's your cousin?"

"Yes."

"How is she?"

She didn't answer for a moment as she changed gloves and retrieved a suture kit. When the needle pressed against his skin, she answered, "Our grandfather has ensconced her inside a lovely compound back in Japan, behind walls eight feet high with more guards than you can imagine."

"No shit?" he asked, wondering how much money her grandfather had to employ such round the clock precaution.

"He's suffocating her, but other than that, she's fine."

Chloe flicked her lovely dark eyes up at him and for a long second. When he met her gaze, odd sensations flooded him, a momentary suspension and sudden downward plunge. His stomach reacted as it had when he'd been on a free-fall ride as a youngster at a fair. The feeling didn't last long, and when she looked back down at her task, he couldn't help but wonder what the hell had just happened to his sense of equilibrium.

She sat back and slipped off her gloves.

"Done stitching me up?"

She nodded. "You have to be careful or you'll tear them. Are you allergic to any medicines?"

"No."

"Great. I have some antibiotics you can take. Listen, I'm not a doctor, but I'm pretty sure your arm will heal if you take it easy. If there's any sign of infection you should go to the ER."

Romeo flexed his arm carefully. "Well, it wasn't a direct hit. The bullet skimmed off something and hit me. I'll be fine."

"You're only saying that because the morphine is masking the pain," she said with a grin. "By the way, I gave you a tetanus shot since I bet you've not had one in a while. I also have some painkillers you can have."

"There's nothing like some great drugs." He smiled.

The door opened and Dax stepped inside. He looked at Chloe with a mixture of longing and mistrust, and Romeo wondered what had transpired between them. Dax met his gaze and nodded to the outside, toward the garage, letting him know that their prisoner was waiting to be interrogated. Romeo acknowledged with his own nod and reached for his shirt.

"Where are you going?" Chloe asked, alarmed.

"To the garage."

"I just said you have to take it easy."

"I know," he said. "But there's a man out there who could have answers to what happened to Babyface, and I mean to find them out."

She pursed her lips. "Well, if you have to force those answers then make sure it's Dax who metes out the punishment."

He cocked one eyebrow at her. "You have no qualms about us torturing him for information?"

She opened her mouth to say something, no doubt ready to pour out all the recriminations shining in her eyes, but at the last moment, she backed down and simply shook her head.

Interesting.

"You have to wear a sling," she told him and crossed her arms. The position pushed her tits out, and even though they were on the small side, he still wanted to lick and suck them.

"I'll wear it if you wait here."

"Deal," she murmured and whipped one out of her bag.

As she helped him put it on, their gazes locked and held. Her natural scent drifted to him, tickling his senses. His dick hardened in response, and he suddenly wished they were all alone so he could experience the delights between her thighs. But duty called. He had to be *responsible.*

He turned and left temptation behind, trying hard to ignore the hard-on he now sported. He adjusted himself before he stepped into the garage, and immediately saw the Shanks member tied to the same cherry picker that Cipher had been chained to not that long ago.

"Where's Mendoza?" Romeo demanded.

The man threw up his chin. "If you're gonna kill me like you did the others, do it quick."

"Others?" Romeo shook his head, perplexed. "What others?"

The man looked between him and Dax. "The other Shanks you killed. Had to be you. Who else would do it?"

Dax shook his head. "We didn't kill anyone. We want Mendoza to ask if he killed one of our guys."

The man frowned. "You didn't do it?"

"Do what, for fuck's sake?" Romeo bit out. The last thing he wanted to deal with right now was a runaround.

"Last Saturday night, Mendoza was found strung up," the man reported.

Romeo glanced at Dax and saw the same type of apprehension on his friend's face that raced through his guts. "Suicide?"

The man snorted. "A big fucking knife stuck a note to his chest, so no, Mendoza didn't hang himself."

"What did the note say?"

"It said leave, or more will be hung out to dry."

"Fuck," Boone muttered. His phone rang and he glanced at it, quickly turning away to answer the call.

The Shank member looked between them. "You didn't do it?"

"No," Romeo answered grimly. "One of our men was killed Saturday too. His body was cut up. The accompanying note told us to leave, or we'll go in pieces."

The enormity of what was going on hit Romeo at that moment, and obviously, it did to the Shank member too, because he began struggling with the bonds that held him.

"Let me go," the man said frantically. "I have to get out of here."

Dax rested a hand on his shoulder. "Just calm down—"

"No! Don't you get it? The Shanks are gone!"

Romeo narrowed his eyes. "What do you mean?"

"Mendoza hasn't been the only casualty. Yesterday someone...or some people...took out half of us. Slit their throats while they slept. Today, most of the ones who survived packed up and left. All that remained were me and four others." He shook his head. "We thought it was you trying to run us out of town. Just let me go and I'll get the fuck out of here, even with a bullet in my leg."

"Are you saying the Shanks are gone?"

"Yeah, man." The man visibly trembled. "You can have this fucking town."

"It wasn't us," Romeo stressed. Several possibilities raced through his mind, but the drug was making it difficult for him to focus on one train of thought.

"Oh, yeah? Well, who else would fight over this town?"

"Romeo," Boone said grimly. All the men turned to him. "That was Hook. Something happened to the Whiskey Lick Her."

Dread washed through Romeo. He looked at each man before they raced from the garage to the front of the compound. Not now. The drug was really playing havoc with his head and all he wanted to do was lie down, but as he joined his men on the road, looking back toward the interstate, the strip of fire lighting up the dark sky made him realize he had a long fucking night ahead of him. He stood with his jaw hanging open for a few minutes, unable to comprehend what the hell was going on.

Dax lay a hand on his arm. "What's going on, Rome?"

"I don't know," Romeo breathed. "We have to find out. Dax, Hawg, Burrito, you come with me. Boone, stay here. Organize everything for a lockdown."

"Wait," Chloe said as she pushed through the assembled group of men. "You can't ride with that arm."

He frowned at her. "I thought we made a deal for you to stay inside."

"I had my fingers crossed," she replied blithely. "If you ride your motorcycle you could hurt yourself more and end up with permanent muscle damage."

Dax nudged his uninjured shoulder and gave him a surreptitious nod.

"All right," he groused. "You can drive me. I'll meet the rest of you there."

All the men nodded. They jumped into action as he marched over to the Mercedes. Without a word, Chloe slid behind the steering wheel and started the car, following after his men who throttled down the road. For the entire drive there, Romeo's insides froze inch by inch as a band tightened around his heart. Someone had taken down the only other gang in Bair, the Shanks, and now it looked as if they were coming after the Men of Hell.

Chapter Eight

Fire trucks and police gathered around the burning building of what used to be the Whiskey Lick Her. A group of people stood off to the side, watching in horror as flames rose high into the sky, soot darkening their faces and clothes. EMTs provided medical aid for several people huddled in blankets.

"Jesus," Romeo muttered.

"Oh my God. Does anyone know what happened?" Chloe asked. The tang of ash in the air filtered through her nose and mouth as it circulated on the wind.

"No. But this can't be a coincidence, not with what happened to Babyface and Mendoza. The Shanks were scared out of town and now it seems like we're next."

The other two Men of Hell members were talking with a tall black man who had on an oxygen mask. Chloe spotted Dax against the smoldering backdrop. As she and Romeo approached, a woman in the crowd stared at them with a malicious grin on her face. Every instinct screamed that this woman had some connection to what had happened, but as Chloe took one step in her direction, the crowd shifted. The woman was gone in an instant.

Romeo had joined his friend and watched the firemen who continued to douse the building with water. Half the building was gone by flame, but it was obvious there was no saving any of it. The Whiskey Lick Her was destroyed. Chloe stood between Romeo and Dax, slipped a hand into each of theirs, and held them tightly, sharing in the atrocity of the destruction.

"Do you know if anyone died?" Dax asked softly.

"I don't know," Romeo replied. "But look at it. How could anyone possibly have survived?"

"I know some of the EMTs," Chloe said. "I'll find out for you."

Romeo nodded. He'd clenched his jaw so tightly, she thought she could hear his teeth grinding together. She tugged on his arm until he tore his gaze away from the scene and focused on her.

"Everything's going to be okay," she told him.

"Everything is not going to be fucking okay," he snapped, pulling away from her and Dax. "People are dead. The business is ruined. The club can't afford this."

"No," Dax said fiercely. "We'll find out who did this and we will make them pay."

"I thought I could do this," Romeo whispered. "The club is sinking and I can't do anything to stop it. Wheels was wrong about me."

"Stop it," Dax muttered. "Yank your head out of your ass and think."

Romeo glared at him. "I'm wallowing in self-pity and you tell me to haul my head out of my ass? You're a fucking dick."

"And you're a pussy if you let a little setback dictate what type of president you are," Dax retorted. "We'll regroup, rethink. We weren't prepared before, but now we know we're under attack. We can even call your brother if you want."

"No," Romeo said. "Lily and the baby need him. I wouldn't ask Branch to leave them."

"The Red Wolves are our allies. North would be more than happy to come himself."

"We'll see. What kind of president would that make me if I cried for help every time a problem arose?"

"This is hardly a little problem," Dax said as he gestured to the ruined building in front of them.

Romeo nodded. "Granted. I just want to try to deal with whatever foe this is before we call in any type of cavalry."

"Well, we know it's not the Shanks," Chloe said.

Romeo glanced at her in surprise. "We?" he questioned.

She nodded and lifted her chin. "I came here to repay a debt. Like it or not, you need me."

He lifted an eyebrow. "Sorry, sweetheart, but I don't need anyone."

"Then what *do* you need, Romeo?" she demanded. "The man I've read about went hunting for the man who fucked over this club. The man I've read about wouldn't moan and groan about how the responsibility is too much for him. You wouldn't have taken the patch if you thought you weren't the right man for the job."

"What do you mean you've *read* about me? Just who the hell are you?"

She lifted her chin. "I'm the person who can fund your club."

He blinked. "Excuse me?"

"You don't want the cavalry, but you need money and supplies to find out who did this, right?" she asked. "To hunt the men who killed Babyface, who burned your bar to the ground? You need weapons to raise the Men of Hell from a two-bit motorcycle club to a formidable force. Lots of weapons. And I can get them for you."

"How?" Dax demanded.

He and Romeo stared at her like she was some sort of freak. It made her want to cave in herself. Hide. Of all the scenarios that had played out in her head, she'd never thought she'd encounter the crazy stare from either of them.

"I have a source," she hedged. She hunched her shoulders, suddenly wishing that this part of the negotiations was over.

"Yeah?" Romeo added. "Why would you help us out? What do you want from me?"

She took a deep breath. Finally. She met his gaze squarely. "I want you."

Romeo cocked his head. "What the fuck does that mean?"

"I want you in my bed. Say...for a month."

Both men stared at her as if she had a screw loose. Well, according to the Psychiatric Board of California she did, but the only way she wanted to treat this tangent was with the object of her affection. Basically, she wanted to fuck her way free of her obsession.

Dax began to laugh. "For a minute there, I thought you were serious."

"I am serious," she replied. "I came to Bair to be with Romeo, and the only way to rid myself of the desire for him is to have what I want. If I have you, I get over you."

"Are we talking guns?" Romeo asked thoughtfully. "Ammo? AR-15s? Fully automatic weapons?"

"Rome!" Dax snapped. "That's not funny."

Romeo looked at him steadily. "I'm not trying to be funny. All we have left are rifles and 9 millimeters. I want to know what the Men of Hell get in return for her generous offer."

"I can get you anything you want," she said quickly. A thrill shot through her at the thought of being so close to obtaining him. "Even a tank, although that might be hard to explain to the local authorities."

Romeo's eyes widened.

"Rome, she's talking about buying you."

"I know," Romeo said. He gestured to the burned-down shell of the Whiskey Lick Her. "I used to be a pimp, Dax. What's the harm in becoming a whore for a little while to help the club?"

"Because there's something not right here," Dax insisted. "Not right with her."

Anger flared in Chloe. She hated to be called out on her crazy, but fighting with Dax wouldn't serve her purpose.

Romeo used his one good hand to grab Dax's cut. "You can't tell me you don't find her attractive. I've seen the lust on your face."

Dax looked at her. Chloe lifted her chin, refusing to show how much her nerves quivered. She didn't want him to know how much his words hurt her. But when their eyes met, that lustful band between them stretched taut and desire flared in his dark gaze. She had only bargained for Romeo, but her body also cried out for Dax. Now she was confused.

"Okay," he murmured. "I admit that I do want her, but she didn't ask for me. She wants you and I don't know if whoring yourself out to a woman you don't know is such a wise choice."

"What if I requested for you too?" Chloe asked quietly.

Astonishment stole over Dax's face. "You want me as part of the deal?"

She shrugged. She hadn't meant to say that. It had just popped out, but she didn't retract it, curious to see what he'd say.

Dax folded his arms. "I'd say I'd feel like second choice. That I wasn't as good as Romeo."

"You could say that," she replied. "But you've felt the chemistry too. I know you have. There's something between us."

He didn't say anything for a long moment. His gaze never faltered from hers. "Why don't you start by telling me where you can get that type of weaponry. Then I'll consider the offer."

She bit her lip. If she told them who she really was, would they turn away? Her family wasn't one anybody liked to fuck with. Reputations were a very nasty burden to shed.

"I thought not," he said, turning away. "Come on, Rome, we have to talk to Hook."

She watched them walk away, frustrated. She'd pushed too soon. Damn.

* * * *

Shantel dialed the number she knew by heart and waited for the other line to pick up. It rang twice before a deep male voice greeted her.

"Is he there?"

Shantel watched Romeo Barrigan from her concealed spot. The big man had on an arm sling and he looked to be arguing with his enforcer, Dax, and some whore. "I am," she said.

"How does he look?"

"Rattled."

The man laughed. "Good. Perhaps killing that prospect wasn't a waste after all. Is Boone there too?"

She shifted her gaze but didn't see the vice president of the Men of Hell. Instead, the enforcer walked with Romeo and they joined two others talking with the remaining whorehouse bodyguard.

"No, he's not here."

"Well, that's okay. The next part of the plan will begin shortly. Once we eliminate both men, Bair will be ours. Good work, baby," the man praised.

"I didn't do much," she murmured.

"You did enough. Come on home and I'll give you a real sweet treat."

Shantel grinned. "On my way, lover."

She ended the phone call and stuffed the cell into her pocket. She'd get rid of it on her way back home to her man. With one last lingering look at the destruction she'd helped create, she walked away happily humming.

* * * *

"What the hell happened?" Romeo asked Hook.

"I don't know," Hook replied. A cut had been bandaged on his forehead and his left wrist was wrapped up. "Drifter and I were on duty and I went outside to call my girl. The next thing I knew, something exploded. Drifter... Shit. He was in there, Romeo." His voice cracked and he squatted in an obvious effort to hide his emotions.

Romeo certainly didn't blame him. Two men inside a week. What the fuck was going on?

"Hey, Romeo," Sheriff Wilson said behind him. He turned around and shook the cop's hand. Wilson had been on the MOH payroll for years, looking the other way whenever they had their suppliers come to town. No doubt he'd been on the Shanks payroll too.

"Hello, Tony," Romeo greeted wearily.

"Do we know what happened?"

"Looks like a gas line popped."

Dax snorted. "That's bullshit. Not with what happened to Babyface."

Tony cocked his head. "What happened to Babyface?"

"Same as what happened to Mendoza," Romeo replied.

"Shit," Tony whispered. "My deputies are still working that crime scene."

"So you know about the Shanks?"

"Yeah. What the hell is happening in this town, Romeo?"

Romeo shook his head. "I'm not sure."

"Six people died tonight," the sheriff snapped. "From what I've managed to gather, two were customers, two were working girls, Candy Box and Drifter. Your people."

Romeo closed his eyes in despair. "The back of the Whiskey Lick Her was targeted."

"Yes," the cop agreed. "There's a shitload more casualties. I don't know if I'll be able to make sure this doesn't interest the feds."

Romeo nodded. "I'll find a way to compensate you."

"Of course you will." Tony rested his hands on his hips and narrowed his eyes. "Does someone want to take over your trade route?"

Romeo glanced at Dax. Yeah, that thought had crossed his mind. "If they do, I don't know who yet."

"I'm still the fucking sheriff of this town. I've got a duty to protect the citizens."

"What're you trying to say, Tony?"

The sheriff took a step closer. "Working with you is what's best for this town, but I can't turn my back on this. Fix this shit, Romeo, or I'm going to have to fix you." He flicked a look around the roped-off scene. "My condolences. When I get the full report back, I'll send the club a copy."

The sheriff walked away, and only Dax's arm on his shoulder held Romeo back from jumping the fucker, even with his injured shoulder. Being talked down to and chastised rubbed him raw, like grinding his dick on a fucking cactus.

"Let it go," Dax told him. "There're other things we need to concentrate on first."

Romeo took a deep breath and turned to his men. "Hook, can you ride?"

"Yeah," Hook replied, standing.

"Call your girl and get to the clubhouse. We're going on lockdown. Hawg, make sure Creole Jack gets to the compound."

Hawg nodded and headed toward the man still sitting in the back of the ambulance.

"What about you?" Dax asked.

Romeo looked over at Chloe, who had walked up to the EMTs to check out the treated patients while some of them waited for a ride to the hospital. This was the worst disaster Bair had seen in a while, and the small town simply wasn't equipped to handle the dozen or so victims.

"I have a ride."

"Rome, are you sure you want to involve her even more?"

He turned back to Dax and sighed. "What if she's telling the truth and she can get us guns?"

"She's still a stalker," Dax reminded him. "Did you forget she's here because somewhere she read about you? Read about you where? And where the hell did she learn to shoot like that? And promising guns? That's not normal."

Romeo snorted. "And what *is* normal? You and me will never be normal, Dax. My parents ran off and left me with a biker club. Yours weren't much better. We run drugs for a living, paying off the local cops to look the other way. We ride bikes even in the rain. We live in a clubhouse behind concrete walls. And we *like* it this way. Chloe might have a few screws loose, but damned if we don't too."

Dax ran a hand through his hair. "It's my job to protect you. Protect the club."

"I know. I trust you with my life." He shook his head. "But we need to start looking at the bigger picture and in what direction the Men of Hell are going. Come on, let's get back to the compound. We need a church meeting."

Chapter Nine

Just as she cleared the gates to the compound, they closed behind her with a clang and a steel wall rolled in front of the chain-link fence. Sentries posted on top of the high towers held AR-15 rifles. The garage bay doors were shut and the motorcycles had been parked safely inside. Cars and people milled about the yard, making it difficult to maneuver very far, so Chloe just stopped and put it in park.

"Come on," Romeo said as he exited the Mercedes.

"What's going on?"

"Lockdown. Everyone's family comes in for protection."

Women with kids of all ages headed into the clubhouse. She frowned. "For how long?"

"Until the threat is neutralized," he replied and marched after the familes.

Chloe looked around at the members scrambling around to get everything in order. She had work in the morning and wondered how the hell she was going to get out.

A little girl ran in front of her, tripped, and went down hard on her knees. She immediately burst into tears, and Chloe knelt beside her.

"Aw, did you hurt your knee, sweetie?"

The little girl looked at her with watery, big blue eyes and nodded.

"May I see?"

She bit her lip. "Will it hurt?"

"Oh, no. Promise."

Chloe carefully rolled up the legging and saw that she hadn't even broken the skin, only scratched it a bit.

"You know, I have a magical Band-Aid," she said, smiling. "It doesn't look like much, but it's very good at healing all boo-boos. Would you like it?"

The little girl nodded.

"Stay here and let me go grab my bag."

Chloe rose and hurried around several people to the back seat of her car, glad that she had her black medical bag. When she turned back to the little girl, she saw that her mother had joined her on the ground. The woman's bleach-blonde hair had been haphazardly thrown into a ponytail and she wore a Harley-Davidson T-shirt that stretched tightly over her big breasts.

"Hi, I'm Chloe," she said. "I was just grabbing my magic Band-Aid."

"I'm Trix and this is my daughter, Marisol," the woman said, smiling. "I'm Burrito's old lady. Are you a doctor?"

"No, not a doctor, but I've studied medicine." She knelt down and opened her bag. She grabbed a bottle of water and a Band-Aid. "This is just some water so we can wash away the icky germs, okay?"

Marisol gave a thumbs-up.

Chloe smiled at her and cleaned up the little scrape. "What a brave girl you are. There, see? No pain. And here's your magical Band-Aid. Leave that on for a day or two, okay?"

"Okay," the girl agreed.

"Thank you," Trix said. She stood then picked up her daughter. "Are you coming into the clubhouse?"

"I suppose, although I have to work in the morning. I just brought Romeo back from the Whiskey Lick Her."

"I can't believe what happened," Trix murmured as she shook her head. "This is going to hurt the club bad."

"In what way?"

"Financially." She shrugged. "Morally. Come on into the clubhouse. You'll have to talk to Romeo about letting you leave. Lockdowns usually mean we stay here until whatever is happening is over."

"Yeah, he explained that, but I work in the hospital."

The club pussy that she'd seen the last time she was here weren't anywhere around. The bachelor man-cave had been transformed into a huge play place for kids to run around as the wives settled in. Some cleaned, some swept, but most stood around socializing. The dire circumstances that had brought them all together didn't seem so dire with all the women and children milling about, and Chloe felt a little out of place.

"Hey, everyone," Trix called out. "This is Chloe, she's a doctor."

A round of hellos greeted her. There were probably about ten women altogether, most dressed like Trix. Each had a certain tiredness in her face or eyes that talked of a hard life, but all smiled their greeting.

"Hi," she said. "I'm actually a surgical technician."

"Which man is yours?" one woman asked.

"Uh. Romeo. Maybe Dax."

Eyebrows went up, but instead of any snide comments the women chuckled. "Well, brother like brother, I suppose," another said with a laugh. "I'm Petunia."

"Like brother?" Chloe asked, confused.

Petunia nodded. "Romeo's brother, Branch, is in a ménage relationship. He, Charlie and their woman, Lily, just had a baby girl a few months ago. I think there's a picture of Ailey somewhere. She's just the prettiest little girl, but her name is certainly a mouthful. Ailey O'Day-Barrigan-Earenflight. Poor thing. She's never gonna to learn how to spell it."

"Here," someone said.

A picture was thrust into Chloe's hand. She stared at a little baby who had light mocha-colored skin, silky dark hair and blue eyes. Petunia was correct. Ailey was beautiful.

"Where are the men?" Chloe asked as she handed back the picture.

"Church," Trix said. "We lost another member tonight."

The women nodded somberly.

"Whatever is happening around here is scary," Petunia said. "I've thought about taking the kids and visiting my mother in Arizona, but Wrench doesn't like that idea. He says he'd miss us too much."

"We need to find whoever is hurting the club," Chloe replied.

A murmur of agreement went through the women.

"Come on, Chloe," Trix said with a wave. "I'll take you to Romeo's room. You can freshen up."

"Oh. Okay."

With a wave at the women, she followed Trix up the stairs and down the hallway to one of the rooms at the end. When she opened the door, she saw a room in desperate need of cleaning. The bed sheets were rumpled in a pile, and Chloe could only imagine the bodily fluids attached to the cotton. Clothes lay scattered everywhere and the trashcan overflowed. A spoiled smell permeated the air, causing her to wrinkle her nose.

She looked at Trix. "Where would the cleaning products be? If I'm sleeping here tonight I'm not sleeping in someone's dried up cum."

* * * *

Romeo was the last man to walk into church. Every patched-in member crammed into the room waiting to hear what he had to say. And fuck if he knew *what* to say, so he sat in his new chair and glanced at each man.

"Drifter is dead," he told them, confirming the news. "So are Candy Box and the Whiskey Lick Her. The last take from Friday night put us at about four grand, but out of that Sheriff Wilson has been paid, plus we had to pay Frank for a decent burial for Babyface."

"So what's left?" Bandit asked.

"Not much," he answered.

He stared at the member who'd been a loyal friend to Shepard. Something shifted in the man's eyes right before he looked away.

"Someone is after our town." He sent a sly glance toward Bandit, but the man didn't react.

"Who?" Sioux demanded.

"Not sure yet. The Shanks are gone, so whoever is trying for a hostile takeover now has their eyes set directly on us."

"And seems to be succeeding," Bandit muttered.

Romeo moved like lightning and fisted Bandit's cut, yanking him up with his one good arm. "You have a problem?"

Bandit looked from him to the other men around the table.

Dax stood watching them. Waiting.

Slowly, Bandit shook his head, and Romeo let him slink back to his seat.

"Enough of this shit," Romeo spat. Fury tore through him and he didn't know where to direct it. It ate at him inside, like a cancer growing in his soul. "We lost two men. Candy Box. Our fucking bar. And we're sitting here with our thumbs up our asses."

"There're only so many places someone can be holed up in Bair," Dax said. "I say tomorrow some of us go out and find them."

"The only other one percenters nearby are the Mutts," Boone added. "I'll call them up, see if they know anything."

"Okay," Romeo replied. "For now, we keep the families here, behind the wall. Safe. Agreed?"

Every member nodded, and Romeo banged his gavel, ending the meeting. The men filed quietly out of the room, leaving him behind. He grimaced as he moved his arm. A soft knock sounded on the door and he saw Chloe standing on the threshold holding her black bag.

"I figured you needed another shot," she said.

He nodded. She'd only taken a few steps toward him when he held up his hand, halting her.

"Close the door."

She lifted her eyebrows in surprise, but she turned and shut the heavy door, enclosing them into the large conference room. She studied him.

"I need to leave in the morning."

He shook his head. "We're on lockdown."

"Yeah, so I've heard. I've been talking with the women. The old ladies." She set the bag on a table nearby, dug through it then pulled out the vial of medicine and a new, wrapped syringe. "I work at the hospital, Romeo. If I don't show, they'll report me missing."

"They'll just think you skipped for the day."

"It doesn't work like that." She wiped the top of the vial with an alcohol pad before turning it upside down to insert the syringe into the rubber top and draw out the liquid. "I have to show up."

He sighed. "Dax and some of the others are leaving to chase a lead. You can leave with them."

"Thank you," she murmured.

He eyed the syringe. "If you're not a doctor, how'd you learn all this medical stuff?"

"I spent a lot of my teenage years in a hospital," she replied. "When I got out of high school, I worked as an orderly then as a pharmacy tech. My schooling was slightly convoluted. First, I got my venipuncture certification, then I went through medical assistance school before going back to study surgical training. I mean, I obviously don't know all the stuff surgeons know, but, truthfully, this stuff isn't hard to pick up."

"Most people would be squeamish at this stuff," he said, using his one hand to air quote the words.

She swiped a small patch of skin on his biceps with the alcohol pad and stuck the needle in. He didn't wince. When she was done, she disposed of the syringe into the red container resting in her bag. Then she checked the bandage covering his arm and secured the sling.

"Not sure if you noticed," she said, "but I'm not exactly the squeamish type."

"Granted. How did you shoot those men?"

Since he'd sat, he had to look up at her. Their eyes met briefly, and she gently, lovingly touched his face. She traced over his brow, his nose, his cheekbones. Her fingertips settled on his lips.

"Have you accepted my proposal?" she asked, ignoring his question.

"How can you get the weapons?"

A small smile twisted one corner of her mouth. "I guess we're at a stalemate."

"We don't have to be, Chloe, but I need certain answers before I can just blindly lead my men down this path. Everything has a price, and although spending a month in bed with you sounds pretty damn good, I can't help but wonder what the *real* cost is."

She teased his lips apart, and he sucked her finger inside. He ran his tongue over the digit, playing. Chloe closed her eyes and gave a little moan. When he released her finger, she opened her eyes to stare at him. Arousal turned her sable eyes into glossy onyx, and the whole mystery of who she was caused his own lust to burn brighter. But then the morphine kicked in and made his dick as limp as a wet noodle.

"You gave me more morphine this time, didn't you?" he asked thickly.

"I thought you could use a good night's sleep," she murmured and bent to press her mouth against his. "I've come so far to be with you, Romeo. You're mine, you know. All mine."

He frowned. The drug was sucking him down fast. "No, I'm not."

"You will be."

"And Dax?"

She sighed and pulled back. "He confuses me. I've never wanted two men at one time before."

He grinned, and somewhere in his brain, he knew it had to be a goofy grin. He really loved this drug. "Luckily for you, me and Dax can please a woman. Together. Like a sandwich. Get it?"

She smirked. "Yeah, I get it."

"Fuck, the world is spinning."

"And that's your cue to go to bed."

He stood, and she slid an arm around his waist. As they left the chapel, Romeo concentrated on getting to his room before he face planted. The stairs were tricky, but with Chloe's help, he finally stumbled into his room and flopped onto his bed. He was only vaguely aware of soft hands stripping him. Caressing him. Lips over his body. A tongue licking his nipples. He was almost unconscious and she was feeling him up. That was depraved and sick, and had the tables been reversed, she would no doubt be ready to castrate him when she gained consciousness.

So why did he like it so much?

Just before he completely fell into la-la land, he thought he heard her murmur, "You're better in person than in a photograph."

Chapter Ten

Vicious stomped into the trailer he and his men were currently occupying, heading right to where the stockpile of liquor set on the dining room table. The smell of sour bodies, sweet marijuana and old takeout permeated the air. He wrinkled his nose. They'd only been there two weeks and already the place had turned into a typical fucking clubhouse.

However, this was not the clubhouse he wanted. He coveted what the Men of Hell had—the compound and the trade route. It was time the Double Guns rose from their place in obscurity and became the outlaw gang they were meant to be. He and Bizerk had worked hard to gather men who agreed with their standards of no morals and even less tolerance, and, finally, opportunity was ripe for the picking. Only two men stood in their way. He'd thought they'd had Romeo the other night, but it had been just a fucking prospect. Still, he had made sure to utilize the dead man's body.

The burning whorehouse had been Bizerk's idea.

He grabbed a bottle of vodka and headed up the stairs, intending to get a good night's sleep. Tomorrow would be their final assault against the Men of Hell, and he would probably stay up all night long to party and piss on the bodies of Romeo Barrigan and Boone Tempest. Shepard had been a fool. He had lacked the vision to hold onto his club, but where he'd failed, Vicious was determined to be smarter, tougher and stronger.

At the top of the stairs, he heard a moan and paused. Another moan drifted toward him. He'd recognize the sounds Bizerk made during sex anywhere. After unscrewing the cap on the bottle of vodka, he took a deep drink. Fortification. He was with *her*. That goddamn bitch, Shantel. If it was the last thing he did, he'd make sure she ended up in some unmarked grave far away from his and Bizerk's empire.

The doorway to Bizerk's room stood open, so he leaned against the frame to watch the show. Shantel kneeled between Bizerk's spread thighs, bobbing her head up and down. His fingers threaded through her hair and guided the blow job. The musky scent of pussy and sex lined the air. Jealousy ripped through Vicious and he had to fight against the urge to shoot her brains out right then and there.

He took another drink, and Bizerk opened his hazel eyes. A shock of light-colored hair fell across Bizerk's forehead, and Vicious wanted to finger-comb it away. Their gazes met. Locked. A huge grin spread over Bizerk's mouth and he waggled his eyebrows at Vicious. He glanced down at Shantel before flickering back up and nodding, giving permission to join in if he wanted.

"Look at my girl," Bizerk bragged. "Doesn't she have the best ass? She's so fucking hot, Vicious. Too hot not to share with my best friend."

Vicious hated Shantel, but she did serve a purpose— one of them being that she let him get as close to Bizerk as he possibly could. So he took another long drink before setting the bottle on a bookshelf and moved toward the ass pointing in his direction. He had no compunction about using Shantel like a whore and unzipped his jeans to bring out his hard cock. One look from Bizerk and he was always hard, not that he'd ever let the other man know about his true desire. In fact, there wasn't a time he could remember when he didn't want his best friend.

Vicious quickly spread her ass cheeks apart, ignoring her squeal of protest. Bizerk tightened his grip in her hair and pushed her back down on his dick. Gagging noises filled the room as Bizerk stuffed his cock down her throat. Some muffled words came from Shantel, but they were indecipherable, probably more words of objection. Shantel wasn't the type of girl who liked surprises. Vicious ran a finger over Shantel's slit, discovering that she was more than wet for penetration, but it wasn't her pussy he wanted. Pussy no longer did it for him. So he grabbed the condom that was on the bed, no doubt meant for Bizerk when he'd had enough of being blown, and sheathed his cock. He fingered Shantel's asshole, using some of her own cream to slick up her hole. Not that he really cared if she was as dry as the Mojave Desert, but still, he needed *some* lube. His gaze clashed with Bizerk's and held then, bringing forth all the unrequited lust he felt for the man, he surged into Shantel's anus.

She let out a scream around the dick in her mouth and tried to jerk away, but he clamped onto her hips to hold her still. He didn't care about her, didn't care if he was hurting her. She was there for only one purpose and that was to be the vessel he needed to breach the gap with the man he loved.

Soon she relaxed under his thrusts, and as he fucked Shantel, Vicious stared straight into Bizerk's eyes. He knew Bizerk loved this, practically raping the chick between them because Shantel sure as hell wasn't having any fun. Like Vicious gave a shit. Bizerk fucked her mouth and Vicious fucked her ass. When they came, it was almost as if they were together. No one between them, no judgment or censure or secrets.

His dick softened and slipped out of Shantel. Vicious fell back, his heart beating furiously. Shantel scrambled away from them, wiping her mouth. She reached for her jeans and hastily donned them, all the while glaring at Vicious, so he flipped her off. When she stormed out of the room, Bizerk chuckled.

"I'm going to have to kiss her ass now," he said. "But damn, that was hot, wasn't it? Love it when we fuck a chick together. It would be even wilder if she wasn't into it."

Vicious wasn't about to remind him that Shantel hadn't exactly been *into* it, but whatever. She was just a club whore and all she was good for was having orifices for cock.

He and Bizerk lounged around, both their dicks still out. Vicious looked at the bookshelf, wishing the vodka wasn't so far away. He was so relaxed he didn't want to move.

"We're all set for tomorrow night, right?" Bizerk asked.

Vicious nodded. "Just after midnight, our man on the inside will kill the lights. We'll get in, rip apart Romeo and Boone then the Men of Hell will be ours."

"Awesome," Bizerk murmured. He yawned. "A great orgasm always tires me."

Reluctantly, Vicious stood. He pulled off the used condom and tossed it into the trash before stuffing his spent cock back into his pants. "I'll let you get to bed."

"Yeah," Bizerk mumbled as he crawled up the bed to his pillow. He hadn't bothered to zip up his jeans. "See ya in the morning."

Vicious grabbed his bottle of vodka, got one last glimpse of Bizerk and closed the door behind him. He wished he could stay, but he'd freak the man out if they ended up spooning. So he did what he always did — he walked away and quickly pushed his feelings aside.

Shantel waited for him in the hallway, her arms crossed over her chest as she glared at him. He so didn't have the stomach for her theatrics.

"You hurt me, asshole," she said. "I don't like getting hurt."

In a flash, he shot out his fist and punched her across the jaw. She collapsed in a heap on the floor, cradling her face. She let out a painful cry as tears poured down her cheeks. Shantel stared up at him in horror.

"I am the fucking boss of this club," he told her. "You are club pussy. You disrespect me again and I'll put a bullet between those pretty eyes of yours. Got it?"

She nodded shakily. He spat on her then took another swallow of vodka as he walked toward his room.

Chapter Eleven

Chloe sat for a long time watching Romeo sleep. It was difficult to take her eyes off him. Happiness and contentment infused every cell of her body and she could've stayed for days just looking at him. She'd done it. She'd managed to find a way into his bed. Granted, he was currently passed out, hopefully dreaming sexy things about her, but still, here she was. Reclining next to him. Touching his face. His body. Surprisingly, he was almost tattoo free. His club symbol rested on his left pectoral muscle and the word 'Freedom' ran down his right side, from his armpit to his hip, in gothic script. The rest of his skin remained bare. A tan line separated his well-fitted jeans from his lower portion. She spread her fingers through the soft dusting of hair on his chest.

She'd never been as glad of her shooting skills as she was this evening. It hadn't been her intention to kill anyone, but a bullet in the right place had certainly maimed the Shanks enough to stop their attack. The idiots may have had the advantage, but they hadn't been very smart about hiding. It'd been easy to find them in the moonlight and protect Romeo.

And Dax.

Why did the club enforcer always creep into her thoughts?

She'd come to Bair for one man, not two, but she couldn't deny that every time she was around Dax her body tingled. With a large sigh, she flopped onto her back and stared up at the dark ceiling. She should sleep. It was more than late and the clubhouse had settled down a long time ago, but restlessness surged through her. She was aroused, and with Romeo passed out beside her, there really wasn't anything she could do. Her vibrator was back in her apartment and she didn't feel like using her fingers when such a fine man lay next to her.

Chloe gave the sleeping man one more peck on the lips before rising. She picked up his clothes, intending to fold them, when his cell slipped out of his pocket. Setting his pants and shirt on the top of a dresser, she scooped it up and dialed her phone number. Her own buzzed in her pocket and she took it out to save the number into her contacts. Happiness flared inside her heart as she laid Romeo's phone on the nightstand, more than pleased that she'd gotten another part of him. Then she left the confines of the room. If she couldn't fuck then she was going to drink. Perhaps a few shots of whiskey would put her out like a light.

The clubhouse was dark. Quiet. Somehow, she figured it was because the wives and children had come visiting. Not all the members were married, of course, and perhaps most of them weren't even faithful to their vows with the club pussy around. But for now, the bar was deserted, so she made her way carefully to it and searched for a glass. Grabbing a bottle of whiskey, she sat on a stool and thought about getting buzzed enough so she wouldn't remember how horny she was.

"Couldn't sleep?"

The voice was like a grenade in the silence, and Chloe almost fell off her bar stool as she gasped and whirled around.

"Shit! You scared me." She covered her frantically beating heart with her hand.

"Sorry," Dax said, although he didn't sound sorry.

The room was too dark to make out his features properly, but his presence was a force of nature sweeping through her. Chloe poured herself a shot and downed it, needing the liquid fortification. It burned all the way to her gut.

"You never answered my question," he said.

"Uh," she managed to gasp once the fire in her throat dimmed. "What question?"

"Couldn't sleep?"

"Oh. Yeah."

He sat next to her, not talking. Not doing anything, really, and soon the silence between them twisted into something tangible. Every move, every breath he took, every shift of his body had the butterflies in her belly swarming and her heart pounding with excitement, even though she shouldn't want him like this. It was enough to make her take another drink. The fire wasn't so intense this time, but the alcohol did nothing to quell the anticipation brewing inside her. It had to be fate that was drawing them together like this.

"Who are you, Chloe?"

The question caught her off guard. Who was she? She was a glutton for punishment, that's who she was. A giggle bubbled up, threatening to spill out, and she sent a glower to the damn whiskey. *Traitor.*

"You were right about me, you know," she said.

"About what?"

Chloe drank a little more and the whiskey fumes wrinkled her nose. Really, the stuff wasn't that tasteful nor was it growing on her. "I'm not normal."

He snorted. "I think we've established none of us is normal."

She mulled that over. No, her life hadn't been, nor ever would be, like the house in the suburbs with kids. Maybe it was the drink, but all the walls she'd built over the years suddenly seemed harder to lock into place. She looked over at Dax. Would it be so terrible to open up to him? Talk to him? Help him understand that she wasn't the psychotic girl the doctors had told her she was? The darkness, combined with the whiskey, helped lower her guard and before she knew what she was doing, the words tumbled out.

"I killed my mother."

Silence — open-mouthed, holy shit silence. She had effectively shocked him into muteness. Sometimes her mouth seemed to work independently from her brain.

"My grandfather is old-school Japanese," she continued, hoping to salvage something from the situation, even if it was just a thread of understanding. "He had a son and a daughter and was determined to make decent, if not profitable, marriages for both. My aunt turned out to have a pretty good arranged marriage. She had one daughter."

"Um," Dax replied, shaking his head. "Kaiya, right?"

She nodded in surprise. "You remembered."

He shrugged. "I was on a run to North Dakota when that whole thing with Shepard went down. Missed it. But I remember Romeo talking about it."

"Kaiya is one of the gentlest people I know," she murmured. "My own parents, however, weren't so besotted with each other as my aunt and uncle seemed to be. My mother was in love with someone else, had planned to marry this other man, until she was forced to marry my father."

"And I take it things didn't go well."

Chloe shook her head. "My mother hated my father. Hated my grandfather. And eventually, she hated me for trapping her."

"She hurt you?"

What her mother did to her was beyond a word as tame as *hurt*, but Chloe had learned how to cope as best as she could. "In ways that wouldn't leave outward scars, but a sadist is skillful at hiding the evidence."

Chloe now wished she hadn't started this conversation. Wished she could sweep the memories under the rug like she usually did, but it seemed like the ghost of her past wasn't finished yet. Now out in the open, it seemed like she couldn't shut up until everything was expunged from her soul.

"I was thirteen when it happened," she said quietly.

He turned his head, and although she couldn't see his eyes, she felt his piercing stare.

"My mother thought of different ways to hurt me the most, and one of those ways was denying me my father. I grew up knowing that my father loved me, but his need for peace outweighed everything else. He stayed away—until that day."

"The day you killed her?"

"Yes."

He didn't say anything. She didn't blame him. Sometimes even she didn't have words for what had happened. But she had survived it. Been hospitalized for it.

"My father visited unexpectedly," she whispered. That day came rushing back to her like a freight train. "He and my mother argued. They were both bitter. She went to the bedroom, grabbed her gun and shot him. Right in front of me. Blood was everywhere. He was on the floor, and I knew I was next, so I jumped her. We fought. I got my hands on the gun. Turned it around. Fired. I killed her."

This time she didn't even bother with the glass, chugging the whiskey like it was water. The amount took away her breath. It felt like it burned away her esophagus but Chloe welcomed the pain. It kept the tears at bay.

"Sounds like self-defense," Dax murmured.

"There was a moment when it was. Then I hesitated and she pleaded, but I still pulled the trigger. I didn't trust her." It took her a moment for the fire in her belly to settle. "My father died in my arms. He needed me but I just... There was nothing I could do."

She fell silent again and the quietness of the club surrounded her and made her skin itch. Sometimes she hated the quiet. It had been deafening after the gun had gone off and her mother's lifeless eyes stared through her. It was a memory that haunted her, so to deal, Chloe pushed it away with all her might.

"What happened after that?"

She took a deep, calming breath. "My grandfather kept me in the psychiatric ward for years, until I learned what to say and how to act. When I was eighteen, I got out and that's when I developed my first tangent."

"Your first what?"

"Tangent," she repeated. "I…developed a fixation on one of the men who worked for my grandfather — my bodyguard. He's the one who taught me to shoot. I wanted to please him so much I slept, lived and breathed my Sig Sauer Mosquito."

"By the tone in your voice, something happened."

"Something always happens." She ran her fingers through her hair, pushing it off her forehead. "I get things confused. I mistake friendship for desire. Some doctors labeled it relationship obsessive compulsive disorder. Others said it was called limerence."

"What's that?"

"It's common among people who experience attachment issues. Basically, I want the obsessive love I feel to be reciprocated. It's a conscious expression of sexual incentive motivation, or so the books say."

He nodded. "Oh. I get it. You think if you fuck Romeo, it'll cure your problem."

She nodded. "Fantasy masturbation only carries you so far, you know?"

"Why him?" he asked. "Romeo, I mean. Was it because he saved your cousin?"

"That's how he got on my radar. My grandfather collected intel on him and the Men of Hell. That's where I first read of the club."

"So this feeling you have for him, it's not real," he surmised.

"It is real," she insisted.

"No, it's not. It's a crush. Simple infatuation. You don't know the first thing about him. In your mind, he's some type of mythical hero you've put on a pedestal. Someone you want to fuck. Possess."

She jumped from her chair to punch his shoulder. "Shut up!"

"No," he said and surged to his feet. He loomed over her, trapping her against the bar. "Romeo is just an ordinary man. His real name is Beau. He pisses and takes a shit just like any other person."

"Stop this," she ordered. She pushed against his chest. Too late, she realized just how big and strong Daxton Squire really was. Then that zing that existed between them, that succulent little desire that wove between them surged to life and all she could do was fist his shirt.

"You don't really want me to stop," he whispered. Dax shifted until one of his legs parted her thighs. "You want this too much. I can feel that hot little pussy grinding down."

She lifted her chin. "I've said no. What are you gonna do? Rape me?"

"Oh, honey, it wouldn't be rape," he said. He leaned down and nuzzled his nose on the top of her head. "Would it?"

He gripped her hips, holding her in place. She tried not to show how much his touch affected her, even when he slid his hands up to cup her breast. He brushed a thumb across a turgid nipple, and the spark shot straight to her core. She couldn't stop her back from arching in pleasure, which thrust her chest further into his hands.

Dax brushed his lips across hers. "Would it, Chloe?"

"No," she breathed.

God, she wanted nothing more than to have his steel-hard cock sink into her wet cunt and pump her until they both splintered apart. But whatever sanity she had left raised a red flag. The timing was a little too soon, her emotions a little too raw. She knew she would have regrets if he fucked her.

But damned if she wanted to stop.

He trailed his fingers down her body to slide under the waistband of her jeans, the touch a little ticklish. Her stomach muscles rippled in protest until his fingers brushed across the part of her panties covering her pussy.

"Oh, honey, you're so fucking wet," he murmured against her mouth.

He brushed over her slit. The cotton-wrapped finger rubbed little circles over her clit. She moaned and jerked her hips upward, bumping against him.

"Oh, my God," she breathed.

"I can feel your heat. It's burning right through this piece of cloth."

He jerked his hand out of her pants and fell to his knees in front of her, hurrying to unbuckle and unzip her jeans. She panted as she watched him, knowing she should tell him to stop, but unable to do so. He yanked her pants and panties down, helping her step out of one side before throwing that leg over his shoulder.

"Ah, honey," he murmured with awe in his voice. "You're so smooth. That's fucking hot as hell."

Using two fingers, he spread her labia and sank his tongue into her pussy. It wasn't exactly the same type of fuck as a hard cock, but his finger thrust inside her, joining his tongue to cross over her G-spot, and she ground her pelvis into his face. She'd always been so easy to arouse, found it so easy to have multiple orgasms, but when his tongue, finger and mouth danced over all her erogenous zones at once, her body erupted in a glorious climax that caught her completely by surprise at its intensity.

"Dax!"

Pleasure weakened her knees. He lowered her leg and kissed his way up her body until he stood upright. She leaned into him, her body flushed with pleasure. His hard cock pressed into her stomach and already desire began pooling inside her again.

"Who are you?" he asked softly in her ear. "How can you get weapons?"

Chloe stiffened. Slowly, she pulled away from him. The darkness obscured his features, especially his eyes, and she wished she could see him, see what he was thinking.

"Did you give me an orgasm in hopes of getting me to talk?" she asked.

"It might have crossed my mind," he said. "But once I had you on my tongue I couldn't stop and all thoughts of seduction fled my mind. Truth be told, it was you who seduced me with your flavor."

He bent his head and kissed her, letting her sample her own musk upon his lips. But her heart ached knowing that not only did he not trust her, but that he had planned to use her own pleasure against her.

She pushed him away and quickly redressed herself. "Well, I must say, out of all the methods of extracting information you could've taken, I'm glad you went for this one. It was much more pleasant."

"I want you, Chloe," he said. "I'm willing to consider your offer. If you tell us exactly who we're getting into bed with."

She sighed and capitulated, mainly because she did want them in her bed. And if honesty would get both men there faster, so be it. "My grandfather."

He cocked his head. "The rich guy who bought you the Mercedes? Just who is your grandfather?"

"Hiro Matsumoto."

"Am I supposed to know that name?"

She shrugged. "Have you heard of the Japanese Yakuza?"

"Yes," he said warily. "Of course."

"My grandfather is *oyabun* to the Matsumoto-kai Yakuza group in Los Angeles," she said. "Basically, he runs one of the largest drug and gun cartels on the West Coast."

"Holy shit," he muttered.

Chapter Twelve

Chloe watched the sun crest the eastern skyline. Tiredness dragged her eyelids down and she chugged the liquid caffeine in her coffee cup as if it was a life buoy. She hoped she wouldn't fall asleep during a procedure because it wouldn't be kosher at all to do a head dive into a body cavity.

Men were moving around as the day started. She'd have to leave soon and sniffed herself to make sure she wasn't offensive. Luckily, the hospital provided shower stalls so at least she could clean up there and wear a fresh pair of scrubs home.

Finishing off her coffee, she then headed back inside to say goodbye to Romeo. Some of the members were leaving to hunt for whoever was after the club, so she had to take advantage of the open gate. Personally, she thought it was going to be like looking for a needle in a haystack for the bad guys, but she knew the need for affirmative action. When Kaiya had been abducted, she flew to Wyoming to look for her personally.

Inside the clubhouse, Petunia and Trix were in the kitchen banging around, and the smell of bacon filled the air. She smiled at the women and headed up the stairs, not bothering to knock as she entered Romeo's room.

He sat on the side of the bed, his dark hair sticking up in all directions. Beard stubble graced his cheeks and jaw. She took a minute to appreciate him in all his nakedness.

"How's your arm?" she asked.

He grunted.

"Awesome," she replied brightly. "Do you need another shot of morphine?"

"Nah," he said in a deep, rumbling voice. "I need my wits about me today."

"You can't ride your bike."

"I know. I'll borrow Sioux's truck."

She dug inside her black bag for her keys, phone and wallet and slipped them into her pockets. "I have to get to work. Will you promise to take care of yourself?"

He grunted again. She smiled and leaned over to kiss him. For a moment, he kissed her back, and a thousand butterflies danced in her belly.

"Okay," she murmured as she pulled back. "See ya later?"

He nodded, staring at her with a mixture of surprise, hunger and cautiousness. She waved her fingers farewell and left the room. As she retraced her steps, Dax filtered through her mind. She wondered if she'd see him and looked around, but she didn't find him. Part of her was disappointed. Part of her was relieved. He'd left her so abruptly after her little revelation that her head still spun.

The gate opened, and she drove out, watching in her rearview mirror as the compound was shut up tight again. She was glad the women and children would be safe from the assholes targeting the club. She hadn't gone too far when the feeling of being watched came over her. It wasn't anything outright and was more of a subtle realization, but she checked all her mirrors and saw nothing. Still, the feeling persisted all the way past the charred ruins of the Whiskey Lick Her, through the small town, and into the hospital parking lot. When she exited her car, she took a moment to look around, but saw nothing out of the ordinary.

She hurried through a shower and changed into scrubs, covering her hair and feet before heading to the nurses' station to see the board. She'd been put into two orthopedic cases, a hip replacement and pinning a broken arm. Bair Memorial was the only hospital with a trauma center for a hundred miles, so they received a variety of cases.

The morning was busy. Chloe didn't particularly enjoy working in ortho because she had to wear a lead vest under her sterile surgical gown. A lot of X-rays had to be taken to make sure the new hardware and screws lined up with bone. After the surgery, she was tired and hungry so she cleaned up her case, wiped down the back table and bed with disinfectant solution and smiled at the cleaning crew. They would be the ones responsible for making sure all the blood was mopped up. Chloe pushed her cart to the elevator and into sterile processing. Then she headed to lunch.

She got her food and went to grab a soda when she literally bumped into Susan. The nurse had come back in a limited capacity, charting and doing minimal work. Now, she stared at Chloe with terror-filled eyes.

Chloe sighed. "So... Perhaps I overreacted a little when you asked if I was crazy."

Susan was frozen. She didn't even blink.

Now it just gets awkward. "All I'm saying is that maybe you should be a little more empathetic to others' problems. Keep opinions to yourself. Otherwise, hope your tongue will be okay."

Chloe turned and walked away—quickly. Just as she swung around, she saw a woman near the exit. Dark skin. Beautiful face. The same woman from last night at the Whiskey Lick Her. Once again, an evil smile curved her lips. Chloe took a step in her direction and the woman hurried out of the exit. She set her tray aside and followed, but by the time she'd reached the hallway, the woman had disappeared. Unsettled, Chloe made a beeline back to her tray of food, although she wasn't hungry anymore.

* * * *

Romeo had stared after her as Chloe had left his room, a ball of energy that he wasn't sure how to approach. Or capture. Did he *want* to capture her? Dax appeared with a mug of coffee in each hand. He held one out and Romeo took it, grateful to sip the hot brew.

"I found out Chloe's supplier," Dax said.

Romeo waited, instinctively knowing that this would change everything. "How'd you do that?"

"I gave her an orgasm."

Romeo had taken another drink of coffee and managed not to choke at Dax's calm statement.

"I didn't fuck her. I used my mouth."

"O...kay."

"I figured we have to be honest with each other if we're going to have a relationship with her."

Romeo carefully set his cup on the nightstand. No way did he want to be holding scalding coffee as they talked about being in a ménage relationship. "Wait. I just met the chick. Who said we want a relationship with her?"

Dax pursed his lips, and that's when Romeo knew there was something he was missing. And that he might not like that missing something. He folded his arms and waited.

"She's Yakuza."

Romeo blinked. "Come again?"

"Her grandfather is head of some branch of the Japanese mafia. So we get in bed with her, uh, yeah, we're in a relationship. Probably for life."

Somehow, without even having sex, he'd fallen into a three-way relationship. For a second, Romeo's brother, Branch, floated through his mind and he made a mental note to call him for advice. And following on the heels of that thought was the realization that he had no business thinking about a relationship when someone was threatening his club and killing his Brothers.

"That doesn't matter right now," he said. "I can't really concentrate on her offer when there's a threat breathing down our necks. Babyface, Drifter, Candy Box. The girls. I don't know who's targeting us, but I won't back down from their offense."

"Good," Dax said with a nod.

"Everything came into crystal clarity last night, Dax. More than likely from the morphine, but I realized somewhere along the line what I want for this club."

"And what's that?"

Romeo stood, suddenly so full of nervous energy he couldn't sit still. He swung his arms around, gesturing in the air. "There are clubs in Omaha, in Kansas City, but *we* are here in Bair. There isn't anyone around with our geographic accessibility. I mean, sure, those clubs could do runs up and down Interstate 80 but we're *here*. Does that make sense?"

Dax shook his head no.

Romeo waved it away. "Never mind. The Men of Hell have the means to be great. Not just a small group of bikers running meth, but a club that lets others know not to fuck with us."

"Are you sure we want to get on the ATF and FBI radars?" Dax asked. "We're small time, easily dismissed, but if we make a play for a larger piece of the pie, we're going to have a lot of people breathing down our necks, and that includes the other one percenters who may not be happy with our expansion plans."

Romeo shook his head. "I want every bastard out there who thinks the Men of Hell can be taken down one by one to know that we are fierce motherfuckers who won't hesitate to kill to protect."

"And just how do you intend for that to happen? We need contacts, money... Actual product."

"I know." Romeo frowned, thinking fast. "Maybe we do need a relationship after all. Chloe's connections are convenient."

"Just think about this, Rome. Be very sure this is the path you want to take."

Romeo searched Dax's impassive face. "You not on board?"

Slowly, Dax shook his head. "That's not what I said. You're my president and my best friend. I will support you no matter what."

Romeo held up his fist and Dax bumped it with his.

"But... Maybe I should tell you the rest of Chloe's story," Dax said.

Chapter Thirteen

The second surgery Chloe was scheduled to assist in went smoothly and she finished early. Chloe clocked out, showered then dressed in a clean pair of scrubs before heading out for the day. As she approached her car, she again got the weird sense of being watched. She halted by her Mercedes to look around.

The parking lot was half empty, but she noticed someone sitting in a dark SUV, observing her. Chloe took off her sunglasses and saw that it was the woman again. Unease solidified into outright suspicion, but just as she took a few steps in her direction, ready to hash out why the bitch was tailing her, the SUV started up and took off. Chloe watched it leave, more than aware of the irony of having a stalker.

As she turned back to her car, she thought of the Whiskey Lick Her. Preliminary speculation had been a gas line leak, but what if...? Shit, what if the woman was somehow responsible? Hadn't she read somewhere that an arsonist usually came back to the fire scene to see their handiwork? So what if this person was following Chloe around because she was waiting for something to happen?

Chloe looked at her car. Was there a bomb on it somewhere, ready to detonate if she started it? Or had she seen *The Pelican Brief* one too many times?

Still, paranoid or not, Chloe suddenly had no desire to ever start her engine. She pulled her phone out of her back pocket and dialed Romeo.

"Yeah?" he greeted.

"It's Chloe," she said. "Can you come to the hospital and pick me up?"

"Why?"

"I just need a ride. Can you or should I contact a cab? Do they even *have* cabs here in Bair?"

He sighed. "No. I'll be there in twenty minutes."

"Great! I'm in the parking lot."

He disconnected without another word. She walked away and for twenty minutes, she simply stared at her vehicle. She felt vulnerable. Stressed. Slightly anxious. All because of the woman, and Chloe did not like this self-reflection one little bit.

Romeo pulled the truck he had borrowed next to her and she hopped into the passenger seat.

"What happened?" Romeo asked. "What's wrong with your car?"

"I don't trust it," she said.

"Is something wrong with the engine?"

She shook her head. "Last night there was a woman in the crowd, not a speck of soot on her, and she wore this proud-mommy grin," Chloe said. "This morning I felt like I was being followed even though I never saw a tail. Then I noticed the same woman in the cafeteria and I swore she was in an SUV, watching me after work. When I tried to approach it, she sped off, but suddenly I got this feeling like I shouldn't start the Mercedes."

"What did this woman look like?"

"Black. Beautiful. Pissed off."

He frowned. "Shit."

"What? Do you know her?"

"A whore, working in the Whiskey Lick Her. She gave me a blow job then ended up punching me in the nuts."

"What? Did she have a death wish or something?"

Romeo snorted. "I don't hit women. Ever. Although I almost went against my beliefs that night. I fired her."

"Seems a little extreme to kill a man over that type of vendetta."

"Yeah," he said. He brought out his cell phone from his cut and dialed a number. "It doesn't fit. I'll send Wrench over to take a look and make sure your ride isn't booby trapped."

"Some part of me knows that's ridiculous," she murmured. "I mean, cars don't blow up like in the movies."

"No, they don't usually blow up," he agreed. "Unless there's a bomb on them."

She frowned at him. "I'm trying to be optimistic here."

He grinned. He talked in low tones into his phone and hung up moments later. She assumed her sedan would be taken care of. As he drove out of the parking lot, he made a right instead of a left, and she looked questioningly at him.

"Where are we going?"

"I thought we could talk, away from the noise of the clubhouse."

"Away from Dax?"

"Him too. He and I talked earlier, about a lot of things."

Oh, boy…

* * * *

"Dax told me about your grandfather," Romeo said as he drove. He didn't look at her.

"I suspected he would."

"Grew up with the Yakuza, huh?"

She shrugged. "It sounds scarier than it was. Did he tell you everything?"

"Yeah."

She bit her lip. "Where are we going?"

Romeo turned onto one of the residential streets. "Wheels' house."

"Wheels. Your mentor?"

"That's one way to describe him. Hold on."

He turned a few streets until he pulled into the driveway of a rather nondescript ranch-style house made entirely of red brick. The overgrown yard and drooping bushes spoke of neglect.

"I just made a mental note to have Hawg come over and take care of things," he said. "This place is starting to look a little old."

"It's nice," Chloe said.

He snorted. "It's suburbia."

"Hardly. I grew up in suburbia."

"Wheels left me his house when he died, but I never had any desire to move into it. I like living at the clubhouse."

"Then why don't you sell it?"

"Because it was *Wheels'* house." He opened his door and hopped out of the cab. He didn't wait for Chloe to follow, although he was very aware that she'd jumped out of the truck and trailed him.

He unlocked the front door and stepped inside. A mustiness hung in the air and her cute little nose wrinkled at the smell. He moved through the house, turned on lights and opened windows. Slowly, the old air dissipated.

"You still pay utilities?" she asked.

He shrugged, not bothering to answer. How could he explain how he needed to keep something of Wheels going?

Chloe walked through the house looking at all the knick-knacks and odds and ends that Wheels had collected. The old man had been a procurer of things, all sorts of things from pictures to figurines to taxidermy animals and beer steins. The walls were covered with that shit, as was every available surface.

"Was Wheels married?" she asked.

"No. His only family was the club. Why?"

"Well, I would've loved to have set him up with whoever decorated the break room at the hospital," she said thoughtfully. "I have a feeling they were soulmates."

"Wheels died in that hospital," he said softly. "Heart attack."

"I'm sorry," she replied.

He heard the sincerity in her voice.

"You were close with him." It wasn't a question but he nodded anyway.

"Yeah." He walked over to a camouflage-covered recliner and sat. "My father was a nomad, and after playing house for two years in Wyoming, he left his son and baby mama to come here. He and Wheels were friends. He hooked up with another club girl and eventually he knocked her up with me. They both stuck around until I turned thirteen. That's when they decided they didn't want to be parents anymore."

"I was thirteen when I killed my mother."

She held his gaze, but he didn't flinch at her words. When Dax had told him her story, he couldn't imagine what she'd lived through. How her soul had survived such trauma. Maybe that was why she grabbed at idealistic scenarios with strange men.

"Why me, Chloe?"

She cocked her head. "What do you mean?"

"Why do you want me?"

"I don't know," she said, shrugging self-consciously. "I read the report about you and…it just clicked in my brain."

"You saw my picture. Were you attracted to my looks? Was thinking I was attractive part of this fantasy you built about me?"

"Not all of it, no."

"You're trying to tell me that if I'd been butt-ugly you would still have pursued me?"

She sighed and rubbed her forehead. "Probably not. But there *is* a connection, Romeo."

"Chloe, look at me."

"I am looking at you."

"No, look at *me*," he said and thumped his chest. "Not as a sexual object, or even a romantic one. Look at the man. Look at who I am. I'm not this perfect man you've made me out to be. Hell, up until the moment I killed Shepard, I thought my life was one big fucking party. Drinking. Pussy. If I wanted to escape, I had plenty of vices to take me away. But now, when I get five minutes to myself, damned if guilt doesn't try to consume me."

"You'll burn out, Romeo."

"Do I look like a fucking hero to you, Chloe?"

"Yes," she said. There was no hesitation at all in her tone or her demeanor.

He couldn't stop the growl and jumped from the chair to march over to her. "I'm just a man!"

"I see the man," she replied. "And I see the fucked-up mess. I see your indecision. Why do you think you're not good enough?"

"Because... Because I don't want to fuck up! Wheels decided to step down and he looked at me to step up, and God damn it, I couldn't. Shepard stepped in and fucked the club. That makes me the biggest goddamn pussy—"

"No. It makes you human."

"See? That's all I am, Chloe. Human."

"I know."

She closed her eyes for a moment. When she opened them, he saw raw honesty shining from the depths of her dark gaze.

"The first man I ever...obsessed over was my bodyguard. I was eighteen and he was forty-five. He saw me as a child and I saw him as someone who needed me. It felt so *good* to be wanted. He's the one who taught me to shoot. Taught me to fight. One night, I seduced him, although, I realize now, having sex with a teenager must have been his fantasy come to life, so I hesitate to use that word. Anyway, I thought he loved me. I began dreaming of him, which led to following him. Fantasizing about a life with him. I took pictures of him when he wasn't looking and framed them on my wall. He was my bodyguard almost twenty-four seven, except once a month he'd go home. And that's when I found out the truth."

"You followed him home?"

She nodded. "I discovered he had a wife. Children. I thought he needed me, and I came to find out he was just using me. I had a little meltdown. My grandfather put me back into the hospital and either fired or killed the bodyguard. I got on meds and back out into the world I went. I moved away from my grandfather. Tried to hide from his reach. He doesn't know I'm here, that I came looking for you. But when he does, he's going to tell you how fucked up I am. How I'm looking for a daddy replacement. But that's not it at all."

With his one good arm, he grabbed her hand and linked their fingers together. "Then what is it?"

"When I read your file, it dawned on me that maybe you would be the one person who could understand I'm not crazy."

Her head bowed and the utter look of defeat wasn't one he expected to see, not from her. She was too fierce for this type of insecurity. He admired her for her gumption, because it took a lot of guts to move to a town simply because of a photograph and a feeling.

He pulled her against his body. When she looked up at him, he placed his lips on her mouth and breathed into the kiss. When Chloe moaned, he slid his tongue inside. Hot. Wet. Lust punched him in the gut.

When the kiss ended, Romeo looked down at her flushed face. "I want you, Chloe. I want to fuck you until you scream my name in pleasure."

"Yes," she breathed.

He planted his lips upon hers again, licking them until her own tongue darted out, meeting his. She kissed him back, running her hands up his chest to encircle his neck. She was such a tiny thing that he stood almost bent in half. He went to touch her, but the damn sling got in his way, so with a muffled curse, he shrugged the damn thing off. Pain lanced through his arm and he winced, but he didn't give a shit about his arm right then. All he wanted, all that kept streaming through his head, was the need to sink inside her body and burn this craving he had for her.

He slid his tongue down her neck, licking and sucking on the tender skin until she panted. Her scrubs were loose so it was easy for his hand to slide up under the top to cup her lace-covered breast. She moaned and arched her back, so he swept the material up and over her head, then she reached behind her and deftly unfastened her bra. He shimmied it down her arm then took a moment to admire her trim little body. Her tits might be on the small side, but her pebbled nipples were ripe little berries begging to be sucked.

He drew one turgid point into his mouth, rolling the nub between his teeth. His arm protested as he slid it around her waist, but he ignored it to pull her more firmly against him. The lust that pumped heavily through his veins trumped everything else as he lifted her up and walked her to the wall. Romeo used it to help hold her up, one hand traveling down to grip the back of one of her thighs to allow him to snuggle in the cradle of her sex. She curled her leg around his back, and his cock hardened even more, wanting inside her tight, hot body. He gripped her ass, drawing her closer.

Chloe cupped his face, bringing his lips back to hers. Their tongues met, intertwined passionately. Romeo wrapped her long black hair into his hand, making a fist, holding her head still. She panted at the small bite of pressure he exerted. At her whimper, his dick jumped, wanting inside her so fucking bad. Foreplay was going to have to wait because he couldn't seem to hold back. What the hell was she doing to him?

She was turning him into a sex fiend right now, that's what she was doing. He honestly didn't know what he'd do if she said no. Christ, he wouldn't ever force a woman.

Luckily, however, she seemed to be on the same sexual pathway, because she clawed at his fly. His senses spun higher and higher. The sweet scent stemming from her arousal made his mouth water.

He dropped to his knees and yanked her scrub bottoms from her body. They fell into a puddle at her feet as he ripped her scrap of panties away. He lifted one of her legs and draped it over his shoulder, giving him an unfettered view of her slick, dusty rose slit. Romeo buried his nose right there, breathing deep. God, could a man become addicted to a scent? One thing he loved was a beautiful pussy and this chick had a Grade-A certifiable, amazing cunt. He separated the lips of her sex, sliding down to her entrance. He licked her, from the bottom of her cleft up, to suckle the clit that peeked out from its hood.

"Finger-fuck me," she begged. "Please, Romeo."

Happy to oblige, Romeo sank his middle finger into her heat. Her cunt was so fucking tight as he slowly slid in then pulled out. Pressing a thumb to her clit, he watched the pleasure course over her face as she rode his hand. He couldn't wait to drive his cock deep inside her. He added another finger to her pussy, stretching her, making her ready for his big cock. She moaned as he returned to sucking on her clit with more intensity. He was determined to taste her cream. She gripped his hair, holding tight and grinding herself onto his face.

Chloe made little breathy moans as he continued his nonstop attack, forcing her to take the deep sensation with limited movement. Her body trembled as she bucked against his fingers. Romeo knew she was close, so with his free hand, he slid it around to her back entrance and used a little of her own juice to slick up his pinkie. Then he eased it into her anus. The added sensation set off a thunderous orgasm in her. Chloe screeched and her body spasmed with ecstasy as he licked up every delicious drop.

Romeo was slightly shocked that he actually *wanted* to lick up every drop. Usually, he didn't care for the taste of cum, but this time he reveled in how much pleasure he was able to give her. As her climax waned and she finally slumped over his body, he stood and wiped his face on his shirt before he lifted her bridal style. She was so slight that it only twinged his shoulder a tiny bit.

He carried her to his old bedroom and kicked the door shut. He flipped on the bedside lamp and tossed her on the mattress. Chloe was naked except for her socks, but he didn't give a shit about those. She lay in repose on his bed, her arms stretched above her head, her body a work of art. Her firm tits thrust out, glistening in the dim light. A sheen of sweat covered her from head to toe.

Their gazes met as he took off his cut and laid it aside. Then he reached over his shoulder with his good arm and lifted his T-shirt up and off. Before he undid his pants, he reached for his wallet and took out a rubber. Playing a little, he did a small striptease, putting a little more swagger into his hips as he pulled off his pants and boxers. He stood naked and extremely horny before her.

"Do you want me to suck you off?" she asked, her eyes half closed.

"No. I want to fuck you."

She spread her thighs and that was all the encouragement he needed. Romeo quickly rolled the condom on and sank onto the bed, onto her. She entwined her arms around his neck, and he nuzzled her with his lips.

He nudged her thighs apart even farther and positioned his cock in front of her sweet opening. Even through the latex barrier, her wet heat burned him. Their eyes met and locked as he buried his dick deep inside her drenched pussy. She let out a wanton scream of pleasure and clawed his back, trying to draw him closer. Romeo had to take a moment and breathe through the urge to climax right then and there. He'd never been inside such a perfect cunt. He pulled her petite body into his thrusts, and she screamed in carnal passion with each deep stroke. He slammed into her little body with all the force he had, and her hot pussy creamed again as he drilled into her.

The bedsprings weren't used to the pounding and squeaked furiously, but Romeo was too caught up in the body beneath his to care. Sweat rolled off him and he wished the fuck could last forever. She continued to moan with each thrust as if she was having trouble forming coherent words. He knew they were both going to have bruised pubic areas tomorrow, but for now, all he wanted was to go deeper inside her body. To melt into her, and some distant thought in his brain wondered how she'd feel without a condom.

Finally, his testicles tightened and his cock thickened. He was going to come. There was no way he could stop it. He only hoped she felt the same way, was right there with him. He gave her one last hard thrust and pushed his cock as deeply inside her as he could go. She cried out with a bellow of rapture just as he let loose, with load after load of cum splashing inside the condom.

He collapsed on top of her, another thing he'd never done with a female. Usually, he pushed himself to the side because he didn't like the stickiness involved in the after-sex part. But with Chloe, he couldn't seem to move. His dick was still semi-hard inside her, and although he knew he had to leave so he could remove the filled rubber, he just couldn't seem to find the energy.

She hugged him tight. God, he had to be crushing her.

"Nothing has ever been so right in my entire life," she whispered into his ear.

And, strangely enough, he believed her.

Chapter Fourteen

Dax sighed as he stared at Romeo's empty bed. He had no doubt where the man had slept last night, and even though he tried with all his might, Dax couldn't push down the jealousy. Not to mention the fact that they were supposed to be on lockdown. The whole purpose of lockdown was that they all stayed safe and guarded *behind* the closed compound doors.

He gently closed Romeo's door and turned to go back downstairs. He needed coffee and maybe a blow to the head because clearly he was stupid to lust after a woman who wanted his best friend. After what they'd shared at the bar, he'd thought they had an understanding. So why was he mooning over her like a fucking pussy? The sound of a truck rumbling toward the clubhouse perked his ears and he went toward the door. As he headed outside, Romeo stepped out of the cab.

"Where'd you go last night?" he demanded, hands on his hips.

"Wheels' house." He held up his good arm to halt whatever Dax meant to say. The other arm was missing the sling. "I know, lockdown was my call. Won't happen again."

"How the fuck do you expect me to do my job, Rome? Jesus Christ, you're always thinking with your dick."

Romeo tensed. His hands folded into fists and his body language gave no doubt that he wasn't scared to kick some ass. "Stop, before you say something extremely fucking stupid."

Some of the members had assembled around them and the last thing Dax wanted them to see was dissidence between the leaders. So he backed down by holding up his hands in a placating gesture. Romeo stormed past him into the clubhouse and Dax followed. He might tuck his tail in public, but in private damned if he wasn't going to say his peace.

"You could've been ambushed last night," Dax said calmly. He figured it was best to take the high road.

"We weren't."

"Where's Chloe?"

"Work."

"She all right?"

"Yes." Romeo frowned. "You're awfully calm right now. I don't trust it."

"So are you," Dax said, nodding. "Have to be, considering we have no clues to the identity of who's targeting us."

"Actually, I might have an idea about that," Romeo said as he scratched his chest. "Chloe thought someone messed with her car yesterday so I picked her up. Had Wrench go look at it. It was fine, but she described the whore from the Whiskey Lick Her who punched me in the balls the other night. And that, my friend, stays between us."

Dax blinked. "Is that a joke?"

"No, but I don't want anyone else knowing some slut got the drop on me."

"No, I meant... Never mind. Why didn't you tell me you'd been attacked?"

"Not exactly kosher for the president of the club to have been felled by a woman," Romeo replied dryly. "Hurt so bad I almost blacked out."

"What did you do to her?"

"Nothing! She fell off my lap, got up, punched me in the nuts. I had Candy fire her."

Dax took a deep breath. He did that a lot around Romeo since his friend had a talent for downplaying everything. "So she followed Chloe?"

"Chloe said she saw her outside the Whiskey Lick Her the night of the fire, then she followed Chloe to work."

"Who is the whore?"

"Name is Shantel, although I have no clue to her last name, and unfortunately all of Candy Box's records went up in flames." Romeo frowned. "By the way, what about funeral arrangements?"

"No funeral arrangements until official autopsies are concluded. Boone contacted Candy Box and Drifter's next of kin. But, I'm sure I don't have to remind you, we have no money to pay for these funerals, Rome."

Romeo threw his head back with a sigh. "We have no money, period. And the Brothers need to be paid, Dax. Some have families and mortgages. Any word yet on that chemist, Red Eye?"

"I don't know."

"Okay. I have to shower, then I have to talk to Boone. We're still in lockdown."

Dax folded his arms and gave Romeo a sardonic glare, who just waved it away.

"Chloe's coming here tonight."

Dax couldn't stop the burst of jealousy in his heart. "Did you fuck her?"

"Of course I fucked her," Romeo replied. "But we're in this together, Dax. She wants us both."

Dax blinked. His jealousy battled with relief that they weren't going to forget him and he wasn't quite sure how to feel about Romeo's casual statement. He decided just to go with it for now.

"So you've decided to take her up on her offer?"

"I have to talk to Boone first, and this has to go to a vote. But... I don't see how we can get the money and the guns we need as quickly as we need them any other way."

Dax had no idea what it would be like to be tied to the Yakuza, but he agreed silently with Romeo. The figurative zip ties on their hands slowly began to tighten. Selfishly, however, he wanted the excuse to fuck Chloe. Perhaps then the memory of her against the bar, surrendering to him, would stop haunting him.

* * * *

After a hot shower, some food and lots of coffee, Romeo felt ready to tackle the Boone and Gabby duo. Sure, Gabby never said a word, but the man was huge and towered over most people, Romeo included. His presence was more than a little intimidating, truth be told, even to him.

They sat in the chapel room at the oval table as Boone pored over the account books. There was a noticeable gap that Cipher had left behind, and unfortunately no one else had much skill with numbers. Boone had volunteered to take on the task, but Romeo knew he wasn't all that comfortable with it. When Romeo sat in his chair, Boone tossed the pen down and leaned back to stretch his arms out.

"Trouble?"

"No, not really," Boone replied. "There's no money, so I'm working with a deficit. How the hell do I rob Peter to pay Paul?"

"No clue," Romeo replied. "We need a prospect or someone we can bring in to take over this accounting job."

"No shit." Boone sighed. "This is a full-time job, let me tell you."

"Have you heard from Red Eye?"

Boone nodded. "He's interested if we can come up with the initial down payment."

Romeo's stomach twisted. Once again, for the thousandth time, he silently cast Shepard into the deepest, blackest pit of hell. "How much?"

"He has eight kilos and is asking for two hundred thousand."

"Shit."

"That's not a bad price. Street value of a kilo is about twenty-five to thirty thousand. With having the Red Eye brand on it, we could double that. If we don't do something, the men are going to start getting restless," Boone said, confirming his own prediction. "We need money, Romeo. I just don't know where we're going to come up with the payment."

"I have a solution, but it may come with a price we don't want to pay."

Boone shared a quick glance with Gabby before cocking his head. "What is it?"

"Chloe is the granddaughter of a Yakuza boss," he said.

Boone looked a little dumbfounded when he dropped his mouth open.

"She's offering weapons, money, the lifeline that we need."

Boone snapped his mouth shut. "So she came here to recruit? How did the Men of Hell wind up on her radar?"

"She came here for me."

"Come again?"

"Chloe is my stalker."

Silence met his statement. He glanced between Boone and Gabby, unsure how to read their expressions.

"I'm trying to wrap my brain around this, Romeo, but something isn't clicking."

"Remember when I went searching for Shepard last year?"

"Yeah," Boone said.

"I helped save a deaf woman, named Kaiya, from his house," he explained. "Kaiya is Chloe's cousin. Their Yakuza boss grandfather had us investigated."

"Interesting. And by interesting I mean—that's fucked up. So Chloe came here to stalk you and keep an eye on you?"

"Not exactly."

Boone rubbed the back of his neck. "Is she legit? How do you know she's not making this shit up?"

"You saw her take out those Shanks men."

"So she's handy with a gun," Boone argued. "That doesn't make her a mafia princess."

Romeo had to concede that Boone had a point. He had never asked Chloe for any type of proof. Was she telling the truth or was that story another one of her stalker ruses?

"So," Boone said, "let's say she's legit. What does she want in exchange for this generous offer?"

"Me," Romeo replied. "And Dax."

Boone and Gabby looked at each other.

"This is about sex?" Boone demanded. "Jesus Christ. You're something else, Romeo, you know that? I've been with this club for almost twenty years. I supported Wheels in every decision he made, even when he chose you as his successor. But damned if I know what he saw in you because all you think with is your dick!"

Romeo surged to his feet. "Watch your fucking mouth!"

"Why? Does the truth hurt? You asked me if I thought Wheels made a mistake about you and I told you that you couldn't waver. So tell me, Romeo, what do you want for this club?"

"I want the Men of Hell to be feared, so no one fucks with us again."

Boone shook his head. "You don't see the bigger picture. You get people to fear us and it makes them determined to bring us down. You make us into something more and we bring the watchful eyes of the feds down on us. We're not Hells Angels, or the Pagans, but we *are* strong men. Good men. We might be one percenters, but that doesn't mean we're assholes who can't care about this community."

The words reverberated through Romeo's head. Over and over he heard the words that he wasn't good enough. He tried to ignore them, like he always did, because he'd be damned if he'd be some pussy-ass club leader who cried boo-hoo. But the words were acid, breaking through his don't-give-a-fuck armor.

"You're holding us back, Beau."

The last words his father had ever said to him. He'd never been good enough. Not for his parents. Not as a man. And now, not as a president. It was his worst fear coming true, and it erased all his strength. He collapsed into a chair, trying hard not to let Boone see how much his words had stripped him bare, his soul broken.

Boone stood confident. Unwavering. He wouldn't have stepped back and let Shepard run this club into the ground. Boone should have been Wheels' first choice. And once that thought took root, it grew like lightning. Of course, that would be the right thing to do. Romeo should have thought of it sooner.

"I shouldn't have been made president," he murmured, staring at the older man. "It should have been you. You've been patched in the longest."

"Don't be stupid," Boone ordered.

He glared at his VP. "Call church for an evening meeting. We have a lot of issues to clear up."

Romeo surged to his feet once more, his mind completely clear and focused. He would get the men to agree to the Yakuza deal, then he would turn over the presidency to Boone. Once Chloe showed up, he and Dax would consummate their agreement with her. This evening, everything was going to change.

Chapter Fifteen

Chloe waited as the Men of Hell guard opened the gate. She'd been glad to hear that her fears about her car were completely unfounded—score one for the whore bitch Shantel. If she ever got her hands on that work of art, Chloe was determined to put a few scratches in the paint job.

Still, throughout the day, she'd looked for her stalker, but Shantel never made an appearance. So Chloe had run back to her apartment to grab several changes of clothes, her toiletries and more ammunition. Next time, she'd be ready for a confrontation.

As she pulled her car to a stop next to the clubhouse, several of the old ladies waved to her. She waved back. It felt odd to have females being friendly toward her. The only real girlfriend she had was Clement, and Chloe half wondered if that wasn't because Clement was still trying to turn her into a lesbian. She exited her car and walked to her trunk to pull out her overnight bag. Okay, it was more along the lines of a large duffle bag stuffed to breaking point, but at least she hadn't brought a suitcase.

The thing was so heavy, though, that it slipped from her fingers and fell to the ground with a thud.

"I've got it," came a deep voice just as a very large hand reached for it. She glanced up to see the vice president, Boone, lifting it easily.

"Thanks," she said. "I'm staying in Romeo's room."

"I know," he replied.

He continued to look at her, study her. She'd always hated being under a microscope, so she folded her arms across her chest, cocked out one hip and stared back.

"Romeo told me about your proposition," he finally said. "You've picked the right time for an ultimatum."

"My motto is *carpe scrotum*. Seize life by the balls." She looked around. "Where's your better half?"

"Trying to figure out the accounting books, since I seem to suck at it."

"I didn't realize motorcycle clubs had an accounting system."

"You thought we're just thugs who sit around all day, drinking beer, doing drugs, polishing our guns and giving the finger at the government?"

She shrugged. "Doesn't everyone think that?"

He smirked. "So why, exactly, would you want to get involved with us?"

"Why would you want to get involved with a motorcycle club?"

"Maybe I like drinking beer, getting high and shooting things."

Chloe shook her head. "I don't think so. Some of these yahoos, sure," she said, waving a finger around. "But you, I feel there's more than meets the eye, Boone Tempest."

"Did you learn that from stalking our club?"

She glared at him. "Listen, I'm not here to upset the club, wreck the club or take over. I'm just a girl wanting a man. My business isn't your business, so unless you're my thong, stay out of my ass."

She gave him the sweetest smile she could muster and marched into the clubhouse. A second later, he fell into step behind her. Several more women said hello to her as she walked through the front room and she smiled and waved, before leading the big VP up the stairs to Romeo's room. He dumped her overnight bag on the bed.

"You legit on your promise of helping the club?" he asked.

"I am."

"What type of Yakuza puppet do you expect us to be?"

She cocked her head, confused. "What do you mean?"

"Don't play games. The dumb, innocent act doesn't really suit you."

"Um, okay. Still don't know what you mean by being Yakuza puppets, but whatever."

"And what happens to this deal when you, Romeo and Dax have fucked each other out of your systems?"

"Don't worry, Boone," she said, patting his arm. "Business deals are *not* personal. Now, if you don't mind, I'd like to take a shower before going down to dinner. I was in a hurry after work and missed cleaning up."

"Don't hurt them," he warned quietly and left.

Don't hurt them? No, she wouldn't hurt them, but she was very afraid that they would end up hurting her by the time this was over. She'd had tangents and she'd dated a few men, but she just knew—call it intuition or premonition—that she could seriously fall in love with both of them. However, she *was* a stalker. A manipulator. Could they possibly reciprocate her feelings? The pessimist inside her said no.

The feeling of being watched, hunted, had stayed with her all day. Every time she'd stepped out of an operating room, she'd been on the lookout for that Shantel bitch, and knowing that this was probably how Romeo felt, maybe even how her old bodyguard had felt, ate at her. She'd never considered what she did as stalking, but the truth of the matter was that she'd hurt people she'd cared about without intending to. Maybe she *was* crazy. Maybe she really did need some type of help. The thought burned like acid in her gut. How could she stomach going back into the hospital when she'd tried so hard for years to escape?

Trying to push away the dark thoughts, she gathered her toiletries and headed into the attached bathroom. The place needed a good scrubbing, that was for sure. Years of bachelorhood had accumulated in all the corners and it more than grossed her out. The toilet seat was up and she used a napkin to lower the lids. The small linen closet revealed some clean towels, thank goodness. Using a clip to secure her hair on top of her head, she hurried to shower.

Chloe secured the towel wrapped around her body as she stepped out of the bathroom, and came to a halt. Dax sat on the bed, facing the bathroom door. He stared hungrily at her, devouring her with his dark eyes, and immediately the butterflies swarmed through her belly. She knew that this was it, that special moment with Dax that would confirm or disprove her little tangent. The night with Romeo was more than she could've dreamed about, but even in the middle of her happiness, she'd thought of Dax.

Had wished he'd been with them as they'd fallen asleep.

"Did you have a good day at work?"

She shrugged. "Today was children. Lots of tonsillectomies. But you don't really care about my work day, do you?"

"Not true," he replied. "I care about you."

She snorted. "Really?"

He nodded. "We're going to accept your offer, Chloe. So I have to know if you still want me?"

"Want you? Let me show you how much you've been on my mind."

Without looking away, she unknotted the towel and let it drop. She stood before him, naked. His gaze raked up and down her body, leaving scorching touches all along the way. Lust turned his face feral, and the thrill of his arousal made her lightheaded. Slowly, she turned around, placed a hand on each of her ass cheeks, and pulled them apart to show him just how serious she was.

"I put this in at the beginning of the day," she said. "I had a feeling I would need to be stretched very soon."

Chloe glanced over her shoulder to see how the knowledge that she had a butt plug spreading her anus, just for his cock, affected him. Dax grabbed the erection straining against the fly of his jeans.

"Is that where you want my dick?" he asked her in a husky tone.

Chloe licked her lips and her gaze fell to his fly. "Yes."

In two strides, he was on her, grabbing her hips to pull her ass to his groin. When he ground into her, it caused the butt plug to sink a little deeper, and she moaned with need. The bulge pressing against her ass

had her mouth watering, but before she could beg, he
spun her around.

"Take my cock out."

She was turned on as much by his order as she was
by the fantasy streaming through her head. She did
what he commanded, but her hands shook from her
desire to please him. She eased the zipper down and
carefully lifted his large cock out of his pants. She had
thought she'd hit the jackpot with Romeo's well-
endowed gift, but Dax just tipped her over into
nirvana. He was long and thick, and the hole in the tip
leaked clear fluid. She collected a few drops on her
finger and stuck it in her mouth. His salty essence
burst across her tongue and left her wanting more.

"You naughty girl," he said. "Did I say you could
taste me?"

He reached back with his hand and smacked her on
one globe. She jumped as fire licked through her ass.

"Are you wet for me, Chloe?"

"Yes," she moaned.

He went from massaging her ass cheek to running
his fingers through her slit. He eased through her
folds to find the entrance to her pussy then slipped
inside, testing how wet she was. She bucked her hips
upward for more, but he left her to reach around to
slap her butt again.

"Get on that bed," he ordered, pointing. "Hands and
knees."

She didn't think. She just obeyed. Chloe was wet
and aching, but she wanted something else beside his
fingers. She crawled on her hands and knees across
the mattress and looked over her shoulder. He
finished undressing then reached into Romeo's
nightstand and pulled out some lube and a few

condoms. She wished he would hurry up. All she could think about was having him inside her.

He knelt on the bed, and the mattress dipped from his weight. He moved beyond her vision and that's when she felt his breath on her backside. A shudder of excitement shot through her. Teeth brushed over her skin and bit, gently, but hard enough to let her know he was there and dominating her ass. Hands palmed her fleshy mounds. Fingers dug in, spreading her.

"What a beautiful sight," he murmured. A featherlight touch ran over her perineum. Her stretched anus. The butt plug moved then eased out. Cool liquid drizzled down her crack. "You want my dick in your ass?"

"Yes," she breathed "Please. Fuck my ass."

The crinkling sound of a condom wrapper had her squirming with impatience. He slapped her ass again and she moaned. Chloe purred as she felt Dax's engorged cock head sliding back and forth over her rosette. His big hands held her waist as he slowly, inch by inch, pushed inside her rectum. Even though she'd been wearing the butt plug for a while, there was still a little pain, but as soon as the mushroom head popped through the tight ring of muscle, the pain settled into a burn — and she loved the burn. The burn had her pussy weeping. She couldn't touch herself unless she wanted to fall on her face, and right now, he still possessed her body. She appreciated him going so slowly, letting her adjust, especially for their first time.

Finally, he was seated all the way inside.

"Oh, God," he murmured, "Seeing my dick buried balls deep in you is so fucking hot. You're so sexy, Chloe. Beautiful. I can't believe you were able to take all of me."

"Please, fuck me, Dax," she gasped.

He eased back, applied more lube and slid back inside her. She was so full, and she could only imagine how it would feel to have him and Romeo fucking her at the same time. The image had her hips moving to meet his thrusts and soon he pumped her with a steady rhythm.

"Your ass is so tight."

His fingers dug into her skin to move her faster, back and forth on his cock. Juice leaked from her pussy and ran down her thigh, and she lost the battle over touching her clit. She face planted on the bed as her fingers found her clit and rubbed quickly. Dax's hands gripped her so tightly that he practically picked up her to fuck her against him. All she could do was grunt and try to keep up with his furious thrusts. The orgasm rose inside her, building and spiraling her upward, and she hoped he was close because she was in the grips of that sweet rush toward ecstasy. Her body convulsed as she came hard all over her hand. Exhilarating. Sublime. And he followed her a second later, shooting his load into the latex barrier.

He collapsed on her, flattening her out, which caused his cock to slide out of her ass. They lay on the bed, panting, recovering. He shifted off her and Chloe turned her head to look at him while her heart calmed. Romeo and Dax had taken her to the heavens and back. Dax drew small circles on her hip with his fingertip, and even though she'd had one of the most intense orgasms of her life, her body surged anew.

"I want to do that again," she murmured.

"Give me a moment. I think you drained my balls."

She grinned. "Perhaps you can drain your balls down my throat."

He closed his eyes and groaned. But the mental image must have given him a jumpstart because his cock began to harden again. She leaned over and grabbed a new condom from the nightstand. He slipped his hand between her thighs to play with her clit. As she turned back to face him, his cock had fully risen. Oh, she loved a man who could keep up with her. She put the condom on his erection then raised up to straddle him. She held onto his dick as she lined up her pussy then lowered herself. He filled her, stretched her, and she threw her head back as her greedy snatch clenched around his thick girth.

"I guess I'm not going to drain my balls down your throat."

"Next time," she murmured.

He palmed her breast and twisted her nipples as she began her ride. Up and down, moving smoothly. Her thigh muscles burned with her controlled movements, and she used her vaginal walls to caress the steel rod buried inside her. She leaned forward, and his cock banged against her G-spot, turning the simmering boil roaring through her body into a volcano. She pressed harder down on him, rode him faster. He gripped her hips so tightly she knew there would be bruises, but she didn't care. He fucked her harder. Deeper. Endorphins raced through her blood and she arched her back, coming again. She cried out Dax's name and a second later, he joined her in bliss.

Then he pulled her down and into his arms, crushing her against his chest. His cock popped out of her pussy and she was sad for its loss. She loved being filled with him. They didn't move for a long time, until he shifted a little and reached down to remove the condom and toss it into the nearby trashcan.

"That was amazing," she murmured sleepily.

"Give me about half an hour and I'll be ready for round three."

She leaned up on one elbow and looked at him. "Or we can invite Romeo and really give my little pussy a workout."

He laughed and slapped her on the ass again, although it was a lot lighter than the previous two.

"Which reminds me, when are you going to call your grandfather?"

She sighed and played with the hair on his chest. "I suppose the sooner the better, eh?"

"Yeah. I have a feeling right now is the calm before the storm."

She sighed, pulled her hand away and sat up. Her bag was on the floor and she rifled through it until her hand landed on her phone. She took a moment to gather her thoughts, organize what she was going to say, then she dialed her grandfather.

"Hello, Chloe," her grandfather greeted in Japanese.

She glanced at Dax and answered in the same language. "Grandfather. I need your help."

He was quiet for a moment, and she could only guess what was going through his mind. "Another situation like before?"

"No. Not another tangent. Hear me out. Please."

"I'm listening."

She took a deep breath for courage. Staring down idiot Shanks minions was nothing compared to talking to her powerful grandfather.

"I want you to release my trust fund," she said. "I want two million in cash delivered to the Men of Hell compound where I'm staying. In Bair, Nebraska. The rest of the money I want in weapons, everything from 9 millimeters to fully automatic guns. Ammunition, flash grenades, basically all the standard fare you give to start out an operation."

"That fund was in place for your future."

"No, that fund is blood money. Besides, I've found my future."

He snorted. "With a bunch of uncouth bikers?"

"You're one to talk, grandfather. I grew up at the feet of gangsters, remember? Oh, and one last thing. I want you to send Kaiya."

"Send her where?"

"Here," she replied. "The club needs an accountant and Kaiya is a whiz at numbers."

"No," he said. "How could you possibly even think about taking her from the shelter of our ancestral home?"

"Home? No, not her home. Her convent. She needs a life. You're not sheltering her, you're keeping her prisoner."

Outrage poured through the line. "How dare you —?"

"She's deaf, Grandfather. Not incompetent."

"She's suffered a traumatic experience. She needs rest."

"It has been a year," she argued. "How much rest could she possibly need? You're making excuses. Don't forget the Japanese quote — *You can always die. It's living that takes real courage.*"

"That's from an anime, Chloe."

"Still a great quote."

"What gives you the belief I would even entertain the thought of agreeing to such demands? You don't exactly have a sound history with relationships."

The statement sliced through her heart. No, her first relationship, the one with her parents, had been rooted in hatred. The rest had been her way of trying to find love.

"If you give me what I ask for, I will forgive you."

His sharp intake of breath let her know just how much her words affected him.

"You forced my mother to marry my father," she continued. "Even when she told you she couldn't stand him. You insisted, and because of you, she beat the shit out of me on a regular basis, killed my father, and forced a thirteen-year-old girl to commit matricide."

He was silent, but she could hear him breathing so she knew he was still on the other end.

"Who I am is your fault, and I've made the best of the life I've been dealt," she whispered. "I know there have been terrible tangents in the past, but you have to believe me that I am where I'm supposed to be."

"You never did back down from an argument," he said.

"You taught me well, Grandfather. You taught Kaiya well too. You don't have to worry about her. The club will take care of her. *I* will take care of her."

There was another long period of quiet. Then he cleared his throat. "I will have the weapons to you in three days."

"And Kaiya?"

"You shall have her too."

He hung up without another word. She'd won. Holy hell, she had stood up to him and she'd won. She wanted to jump up and down, or twirl around... Do *something* to memorialize the moment. Chloe didn't even realize she was crying until Dax wiped the tears from her cheeks.

"You okay?"

She nodded and smiled. She wasn't the girly girl who would jump or twirl in glee. "Three days. Everything will be here then."

"Thank you, Chloe," he said. He ran a finger over her cheek. "Having you will make it worth being under a Yakuza thumb."

She frowned. "Boone mentioned something similar. Dax, I'm not asking you to join the Yakuza. Not unless you want to. This offer is strictly from me."

Several emotions filtered through his eyes until he managed to mask them. She wasn't quite sure what he thought of her offer now, but damned if she could stop it. The hand had already been played. But she knew one way to take his mind off things.

She fell to her knees in front of him. His cock was already hard again and she peeked at him through her lashes. "Half hour my ass."

He grinned. "I've had that ass. I'll do that ass anytime."

"And I like this cock." She licked the head and tasted a drop of his salty pre-cum. "Yum."

He groaned and buried his hands in her hair. It didn't take much to guide her mouth to suck his cock. She happily swallowed him down. Chloe didn't understand a lot of girls who said they didn't like giving head or being fucked in the ass. She couldn't imagine two better ways to pass the time, unless it was waiting for Romeo to join them for a *ménage à trois*.

"Suck me, sweetheart," Dax moaned. "Holy fuck, that feels good."

Chloe held the base of his cock so she could better suck on him and she began the blow job with short, shallow thrusts. Each time she took him into her mouth, she eased her throat muscles a little more. Allowing his cock to go farther, deeper took practice since her mouth was small, so she had to work up to deep-throating, but Dax didn't seem to mind the wait.

He was moaning, the involuntary thrust of his hips shallow and stilted.

Little by little, Chloe increased the tempo, sucking him harder—faster. She squeezed Dax's sac, gently rolling the balls. Dax gave a heavy gasp, his hips twitching under the restraint he held.

"Fuck!" he grunted. "I should be able to last, but your mouth is heaven. I'm going to come."

Satisfaction rolled over her. There was nothing quite like causing a big, strong man like Daxton Squire to lose control. She continued her assault, not moving her mouth off him or slowing her rhythm. With one more slide of her tongue, he exploded, shouting out his pleasure. She swallowed down his cum, milking him for every drop he spewed. After a few moments, Dax slumped, and she pulled off, using the nearby sheet to wipe her mouth. Guess she was going to have to do laundry again.

When he had managed to get his breathing under control, he hauled her up and into his arms. She rested her head upon his chest and heard the steady rhythm of his heart. And damned if it didn't make her heart beat with some type of emotion she'd never felt before. What it was, she didn't know. She only knew she liked it and wanted more of that contented feeling.

Chapter Sixteen

Romeo sat in his chair, watching the men file into the room. Dax was the last, finger-combing his wet hair—and he knew why. Romeo had known he was in his bedroom with Chloe, and he'd deliberately stayed away. To make this thing between them work, they had to have some time to themselves. He'd waited for jealousy to kick in but, surprisingly, all he felt was hope that Dax was as connected with Chloe as he was.

He banged his gavel and brought the meeting to order.

"Where's Bandit?" he asked.

"Shitter," Boone replied.

Romeo nodded. "Well, someone can catch him up. There are several issues that need to be addressed," he said. "We have a good lead on Red Eye, who says he has something special for us. He's willing to sell us eight kilos of his new powder for two hundred grand."

Murmurs broke out among the members.

"We can net a pretty good profit even keeping our regular territories," Boone replied. "But we have to trust the reliability of his brand."

"I thought we didn't have any money," Sioux said, addressing the rumblings.

"We don't," Romeo replied. "Yet. But I have a proposition to bring to the table, one that alleviates that particular pressing need."

"Let's hear it," Hook demanded.

"I'm sure you all know Chloe," Romeo said, looking around the table. The men nodded. "She's the granddaughter of a Yakuza boss. She's offered to give us weapons and cash."

Shocked silence encompassed the table.

"I'm bringing this to a vote, because if we all agree, we're looking at being Yakuza subjects—"

"No, we're not," Dax interjected.

Romeo frowned. "What?"

"Chloe is offering this on her own. I talked to her earlier. Her grandfather is supplying the guns, of course, but only with her money."

All the men glanced at each other. Romeo felt as if someone had punched him extremely hard in the stomach. Her money? How much fucking money did she have? And how the hell did he feel about her having enough money to fund the Men of Hell?

"What's the catch?"

Dax shook his head. "No catch. She's…" He looked at Romeo, their eyes met and held. "She's me and Romeo's old lady."

Jaws dropped. A shocked silence drifted through the room, and one side of Romeo's mouth curled up. *Well, shit. I have an old lady.* Wait, did that mean Dax was his old man? No, that was too fucked up. He was going to have to call Branch about this, not that he was opposed to suddenly losing his bachelorhood. Dax had stated what had been swimming through his own head, a half-formed idea that had slowly been taking root ever since his and Chloe's night together in Wheels' house. But relationships were hard work to begin with, so adding in another member was going to make life interesting.

If she's rich, does this make me her boy toy?

"I guess your older brother was a bad influence," Boone remarked dryly.

Everyone laughed.

Romeo let them have their moment to poke fun because he was confused as hell. Was he supposed to be happy? Accepting? He really didn't have time to deal with this right now, so he pushed all his personal thoughts to the side.

"All right, rein it in," Romeo ordered sharply. "I suppose that takes one thing off the agenda."

"And relieves my mind," Boone added. "No offense, but I personally didn't want to be a Yakuza bitch."

Romeo silently agreed. "Although I like my bitch," he said.

"You'd better not let Chloe hear you call her that," Dax warned. "Because I think she knows how to tie nuts in a knot."

Several of the men winced.

Romeo glanced around the table, knowing that this was the time to bring up the change of leadership topic. He stared at the gavel in his hand and wondered how he'd feel watching Boone bang it to bring a meeting to order. Wheels had often told him that ownership of the gavel was a combination of leader, peacekeeper and politician, and now that he was so close to giving it up, something inside him seized.

He cleared his throat and forced himself to push the words out.

This was the right thing to do. Not for him, but for the club.

"You're holding us back, Beau."

"You can't waver, Romeo."

"I need to bring up something else, something... different from Wheels' vision of who should sit at the head of this table."

Dax frowned. Boone frowned.

He opened his mouth to continue, and the lights suddenly went out. And it wasn't just in the chapel. Screams and yelling came from the front of the clubhouse, where the women and children gathered in the evenings after dinner.

"What the fuck?" Romeo surged to his feet, but everything was pitch dark and he hit his knee against the table.

A couple of members pulled out their phones to give them light. They all hurried from the room, toward the front. Some of the women had found flashlights and candles. Romeo didn't know they even *had* candles.

"Power outage?" Dax asked.

Romeo could tell from the suspicion in his voice that he didn't think so. Neither did Romeo.

"Get the families to the bomb shelter," he ordered, thinking quickly. "Tell the old ladies they're going to have to deal with the sweet butts. Have Burrito and Hook go with the women and children to protect them."

Dax nodded and left to follow the directives. Romeo turned to Boone and Gabby.

"Take a few men and check the perimeters," he said. "Make sure I'm just being paranoid."

"On it," Boone replied.

"Wrench," he addressed. "Take Hawg and go check the generators and see why they aren't kicking in."

"Okay," Wrench said and hurried away.

"Sioux," he called out as he moved to the door. "Come with me to the munitions storage so we can distribute what guns we have."

The Native American man followed him. They headed across the murky compound quickly. Romeo didn't like that every glimmer of light seemed to have been extinguished. Even thick clouds obscured the moon. Glowing lights flashed through the blackout, and sometimes the bright screen of a phone cut through the night. He and Sioux had just reached the storage unit when gunfire erupted. Romeo ducked down and hurried to the side, trying to find any type of cover, and he felt Sioux dive beside him.

"What the fuck?" He pulled his 9 millimeter from its shoulder holster under his cut.

"I see several flash points," Sioux muttered. "God damn it, how did they get in?"

From his vantage point, he couldn't answer the question. But the majority of the firing came from the direction of the gate, and that left a cold feeling in the pit of his stomach. "Listen, the combination to the storage unit is forty, thirty, twenty-one. Get it open and distribute the guns."

"Yes, boss."

Romeo focused on one origin flash as gunfire again erupted through the night. It seemed like the assholes were aiming at the clubhouse and he was glad he had the families moved. But Sioux had asked a very important question.

How in the hell *had* they got in?

The one advantage he had over the fucking attackers was the fact that he knew every square inch of the compound, and he utilized that knowledge by maneuvering silently to the gunman closest to him. A mound of tires separated him and the person shooting, and when he heard the click of the hammer, Romeo realized his opportunity. He didn't want to kill the person right away. He wanted to know who the fuck was trying to take them out.

Romeo charged and barreled into the man, sending them both to the ground. The first thing he realized was that the attacker was wearing night-vision goggles and quickly yanked them off. Disoriented, he tried to fight blindly, but Romeo blocked his punches, reared back with his own fist and bashed it into the man's face. He grunted and fell. Romeo pressed the barrel of his gun against the fucker's forehead.

"Who are you?" he demanded.

"Fuck you," the man gasped.

Romeo aimed his gun and shot him in the hand. A blood-curdling scream left his lips and the warm spatter of blood hit Romeo's face. He placed the gun's barrel back on his forehead and the man gasped when the hot metal seared the skin.

"I'll be happy to shoot off all your extremities," Romeo said coldly. "Tell me who the hell you are and I'll consider not doing that."

"T-The D-D-Double Guns."

"What do you want?"

The asshole only groaned.

Romeo grabbed the other hand and pushed his gun into it.

"No!" the man cried. "Bair! We want the town. And Vicious wants Romeo and Boone dead."

"Vicious?"

"Yeah. Vicious and Bizerk run the club. That's it, I swear. That's all I know."

"Noted," Romeo replied and shot the poor sap in the head. He felt no remorse for killing anyone who had invaded and shot ruthlessly into a house that had been full of women and children. Relief that he'd gone with his gut to get them to the bomb shelter made him more determined to hunt the fuckers down and destroy them.

Besides, they had killed Babyface, Drifter and Candy Box. They weren't exactly even, but this certainly helped alleviate some of his vengeful rage.

The shooting was still going on, but as Romeo got off the dead informant, he noticed from the angle and sound of the gunfire that Sioux must have distributed the weapons because his Brothers were fighting back with the rifles.

Just as he picked up the dead man's night-vision glasses, the floodlights at the four corners of the compound flared to life, bathing the grounds in bright light. He squinted, trying to find everyone.

The sudden light brought a quick ceasefire, probably because the invaders were blinded from wearing the night goggles, screaming in agony. Bullet holes peppered the clubhouse—so many he couldn't count them all. Romeo saw several MOH Brothers in the broken windows on the second floor keeping watch and he thought about Chloe. She'd been upstairs. At least, that's where he figured she'd been when Dax had come hurrying late to the church meeting. Although panic tried to raise its head, he pushed the freezing feeling aside to focus on what had to be done. Besides, Chloe knew how to take care of herself.

That's what he had to believe, because if anything happened to her... Jesus, he fucking hoped nothing had happened to her. Just as that thought formed, an agonizing cry roared over the sudden silence, followed by a single gunshot, and Romeo's heart skipped a beat.

* * * *

At the first sound of gunfire, Chloe rolled out of bed and crouched down. Naked, she shimmied her way over to the discarded clothes on the floor and dressed while lying down. It took her a moment to remember where she'd put her gun, and found it in her medical bag. She slipped a few extra magazines in her jeans pockets.

Romeo's bedroom faced the back of the clubhouse, and as she made her way out of the room, she realized that all the firepower seemed concentrated on the front of the building. Several stray shots flew through the windows to puncture the hallway walls. She stayed low and moved fast. The last thing she planned on doing was dying that night.

She had to follow the curses of the men since the pitch darkness prevented her from seeing anything. Her memory led her out the back. Where was Romeo? And Dax? All she focused on was finding them, making sure they were okay, because if they were shot... Dead... Her heart stuttered in her chest as her stomach flip-flopped.

No, don't think about that.

Chloe kept to the shadows and hoped that none of the Men of Hell mistook her for one of the bad guys. She couldn't see much in the oppressive night that covered the compound. They were too far away from civilization to catch any of the town lights. Logically, to get the drop on them, the power had to be cut and the sentries taken out. She made her way toward one of the towers where the members took turns standing guard to watch the gate. It was the direction from which the attack had come, so she pushed forward, instinctively feeling that that was where Romeo would head.

When a shadow moved toward her, she ducked behind a shed, circling until she leveled her gun at the intruder. She saw the person wore night-vision goggles. It didn't surprise her because this was obviously a meticulously planned attack, bold and organized, and the idea of treachery swam in her thoughts.

"Stop," she ordered.

The person froze.

Around them shouts from both sides sounded, adding to the thunderous cracks of the guns. Chloe ignored them as she took a step closer to make sure her aim in the dark was true. The person suddenly spun and kicked upward, snapping her hand and causing her to lose her grip. Her gun dropped, but Chloe couldn't focus on it. The intruder aimed the semi-automatic. Chloe shoved the gun up as it fired, using her body weight against the attacker. As they fell, she landed on top of the person and the soft breasts that cushioned her fall revealed with whom she wrestled. In one quick move, she ripped off the hood and goggles. Even in the dark, she could tell it was the bitch Shantel. The woman flinched and blinked rapidly to clear her eyesight.

"I thought I smelled something whorish," Chloe taunted.

"Get off me," Shantel demanded.

"Why were you following me? What are you trying to do?"

Shantel's fist flew up, catching her off guard, and Chloe fell back. She grabbed her jaw as she scrambled to her feet. Just as Shantel bent to pick up her gun, Chloe kicked it away. They stood face to face, circling each other.

"I know who you are," Chloe said.

"Oh, really? You know I'm the girl who sucked off your man?"

"And now I know you're the girl whose ass my foot is going into."

Shantel snorted and pulled a knife out from behind her.

Chloe shrugged. "I've had worse odds. Shall we test the disadvantage?"

"I don't think that's going to be very fair, do you?"

"I'm willing if you are."

The weapon was a small thing that gleamed dully. Shantel struck out, swiping the blade, and had Chloe not been prepared and ducked back, it would have sliced her face. Shantel advanced, jabbing with the knife, but each time Chloe managed to avoid being stabbed. She knew her luck would eventually run out, though, so on the next swing, she went on the offensive. As it arched upward, Chloe dodged away, falling to the ground and rolling right into Shantel's legs. Shantel lost her balance, hitting the ground hard with a strangled gasp.

Chloe didn't give her time to recover, straddling her and punching her in the face. Shantel groaned as she let go of the knife. Chloe scooped it up and held it to the woman's throat.

"Why have you been attacking the Men of Hell?"

Shantel spat at her. Chloe wiped the trickle of spit off her face. Then she backhanded her. Shantel's head snapped to the side, but other than licking the trickle of blood that dribbled down her chin from the blow, she didn't even flinch.

Suddenly, Shantel bucked beneath her, and a pair of knees hit her spine. Caught off guard, Chloe jerked forward, the edge nicking Shantel's throat, but the other woman didn't seem to care. She wound her arms around Chloe's chest, tossing her off.

The knife slipped from her hand and lay between them. Chloe didn't waste a second, lunging for it at the same time as Shantel. Shantel used her bigger body as a bumper car, barreling into Chloe in an effort to knock her even more off center. But Chloe had learned how to fight dirty because most opponents were bigger than her, so she twisted and used Shantel's own height against her to bring her down. They fell into a pile of arms and legs, with the blade a power struggle between them.

"I'm going to kill you," Shantel raged at her.

"Fucking bitch, let go of me!"

Chloe rolled and a second later, Shantel grunted in her ear. Chloe felt the tip sink into flesh and knew that Shantel had been stabbed, only she didn't know how deeply. She wrenched it out wherever it had impaled and ribbons of blood splattered against Chloe's cheek. Chloe realized Shantel had been injured pretty bad. She scrambled to her feet and held the knife sure and steady in her hands, waiting for any type of return attack.

Suddenly, the lights blazed to life and Chloe saw the unblinking gaze of Shantel staring up into the heavens. Dead. A big, bloody wound covered the center of her chest.

"No!"

Chloe spun. A man stood not too far away, staring in absolute disbelief and shock at the lifeless body on the ground. He must have pulled off his goggles earlier because they tumbled from his hand to the ground. He turned hate-filled eyes her way, staring at the blood-tipped knife she still gripped in her hand, and raised his gun. She sucked in a deep breath, bracing for the impact of a bullet, and a shot went off. Chloe jerked in response, and it took a moment for her brain to catch up to the fact that she wasn't in pain and she wasn't bleeding. Another man rushed forward to yank on the downed man's arm while leveling his own weapon on her.

"Come on," the second man muttered as he tugged on the first guy's arm. "Our advantage is gone."

Romeo marched out, a pistol in each hand, his face set in a cold mask of determination.

"I'll shoot her!" the second man yelled.

"No, Romeo, he'll kill her!" Dax shouted.

Romeo halted. His aim never wavered. "Are you Vicious?"

The man lifted his chin.

Chloe took that as a yes.

"You kill him and I'll kill her," Vicious said. "So keep your woman breathing, you're going to let us walk away."

Hatred lined every surface of Romeo's face, but he nodded.

"You take your men and get out of here with the knowledge that as soon as my men have been treated, I am going to hunt your ass down and kill you," he vowed.

Through all this, the first man never took his hate-filled gaze off her, and Chloe knew if she believed in fate, she was staring at her death. Vicious managed to convince him to leave, and they, along with their men, backed up until they were out of the gate. One of the men rolled it shut, and once again, they were back behind a fortified wall.

She turned and sprinted to Dax and Romeo. A moment later, she was in their embraces and she hugged them both tightly, relishing the fact that they were both with her — and unhurt.

Chapter Seventeen

Dax watched Chloe work on the wounded. She'd already declared that two had to be taken to the hospital, so they'd called the sheriff. He'd find out anyway since gunshot victims were immediately reported. As he looked around, he didn't see Hawg or Wrench, so he headed toward the shack that held the back-up generator.

It was located in the upper north corner of the compound, and as he approached, his gut tightened, the type of warning he'd learned to heed over the years. He palmed his pistol once more and stood to the side as he slowly pushed the door open. Wrench lay propped on against the wall, holding his bleeding stomach. Next to him lay Hawg, seemingly unconscious, and on the other side of the generator was Bandit. There was absolutely no doubt that he was dead since a bloody, round hole lay in the middle of his forehead.

"He...he sabotaged the generator," Wrench whispered. "Hawg and I caught him breaking it. He hit Hawg. He shot me. I shot him."

"And you fixed the lights."

"Yes."

Dax pulled out his cell and called Chloe.

"Dax?" she questioned.

"Get to the generator shed. Wrench has been gut shot."

"On my way."

She hung up. Dax bent to check Hawg. The man moaned and stirred, so he knew he would be okay, but Wrench had him worried. And by the weary look in Wrench's eyes, the man knew his wound was serious.

A moment later, Chloe rushed into the small shack with her medical bag. She fell to her knees beside Wrench and pulled on some gloves before gently probing his belly.

"He needs to get to a hospital, ASAP," she said grimly. She opened a large package that said 'Sterile' on it and put the gauze over the bleeding wound. Then she placed one of his hands on top of it. "Hold this as tightly as you can, okay?"

"Okay," Wrench whispered.

Hawg groaned and sat up. He looked around and his attention landed on Wrench. "Oh, shit!"

Chloe walked over to him and squatted to shine a flashlight in his eyes. "Any dizziness? Blurred vision? Your pupil response looks fine."

"No," Hawg said. "I'm just pissed off that asswipe got the jump on me."

"Then would you mind directing the ambulance here as soon as it arrives?" she asked. "Out of everyone, Wrench's wound needs to be addressed immediately."

"Am I gonna die?" Wrench asked.

Chloe shook her head. "Of course not. Dax, why don't you make arrangements for Petunia to come wait with him?"

"No," Wrench mumbled. "I don't want to...to worry her."

"Well, I don't want to face her wrath when she learns I sent her husband to the hospital and didn't tell her," she said dryly. "Would you?"

One side of his mouth crooked upward in a semblance of a grin and he shook his head.

Dax pulled out his cell and made a call while Hawg left to go wait for the ambulance. Wrench raised his hand toward her and Chloe grabbed it, holding tight.

"Wrench?"

"I need you to tell Petunia something for me—"

"Shh," Chloe said. "No death bed confessions allowed. You're going to the hospital because you need emergency surgery, but I'll be with you, Wrench. Okay? I'll ask to scrub in so I can make sure you get the best care."

Wrench nodded, but his face scrunched up into a grimace. Dax hated to see his Brother suffering.

He hung up his call. "Hook is escorting Petunia. She should be here any minute."

"See?" Chloe said, smiling at Wrench. "You can tell her whatever it is yourself."

A second later, his wife, Petunia, rushed inside. She took one look at the scene, at the dead man, at her husband with blood all over his belly, and she emitted a little distressed cry.

"I got a hole in my new T-shirt," Wrench said then coughed.

"Well, now it matches all your others," Petunia replied softly as she smoothed the hair around his face.

EMTs entered the now-cramped space, and Dax took hold of Chloe's arm and maneuvered them both out of the way. Except for a quick check to see if Bandit needed any help, the two men seemed focused. They worked on Wrench, asking questions, taking vitals. It seemed to take forever before they finally loaded him onto a stretcher and many times Dax wanted to threaten them with bodily harm. But then Petunia was following them into the ambulance, leaving Dax and Chloe standing in the small shed with a corpse at their feet.

And not just any dead body — a traitor — one of their own.

"I have to go," Chloe said. "I have to get to the hospital so I can ask to scrub in."

Dax took her into his arms and kissed her, hard. There was no passion behind the gesture, only the taste of desperation. They both could have lost their lives tonight and suddenly the thought of not having her around, of something devastating happening to her, filled him with a sense of dread. He watched her walk toward the ambulance and talk with the driver before sliding into the passenger seat. Just as the ambulance left the compound, the sheriff's car drove in. He sighed. It was going to be one hell of a long night.

Chapter Eighteen

"I want that bitch dead!"

Bizerk paced back and forth in the small living room with a bandage covering part of his face. Vicious was glad that the bullet had only grazed him. He didn't know what he'd do if something happened to Bizerk. The remaining men of the Double Guns sat around, waiting for the next move. Vicious drank a beer and watched his partner, silently applauding the spitfire who had finally had the strength to kill Shantel. Bizerk had been in love, but Vicious hated the cunt, mainly because Bizerk loved her. He hadn't wanted her on the raid, but Bizerk had thought she'd be an asset. Now, he was extremely glad she'd been in the right place at the right time to get herself killed.

"You should be focused on how our foolproof plan was anything but," he commented. "How the hell did they regain control of the generator?"

Bizerk spun and marched up to him, standing nose to nose. "My girl is dead, Vicious! How can I possibly care about what the hell happened?"

"Because we don't want it happening again, do we?"

"I want that Chink dead," he repeated, his tone flat and absolute.

"Fine. Let's think about our next move, and I promise you can have first dibs on killing the Asian bitch."

Bizerk nodded and resumed his pacing. "They'll probably be at the hospital. We should attack there."

"What, now?"

Bizerk shrugged. "Why not? They won't be expecting it. What they will expect is for us to lick our wounds and give them enough time to gather their strength. You heard Romeo, he's going to come gunning for us. This way we can keep them off guard."

Vicious thought about what was probably happening at the Men of Hell compound. He had no doubt that Romeo now knew who was behind all the attacks. He'd lost three men tonight, not including Bandit, his inside spy. It had been Bandit's job to cut the power and make sure the backup power generator couldn't be restarted, giving them the tactical advantage with the night-vision goggles. And since the floodlights had come on, well, losing Bandit was a huge loss to his plans. When he'd met the man in a bar in Omaha, he'd taken it as a sign that it was time to leave his club and start his own. Bandit had painted a good picture. An *easy* picture. Just eliminate the two men running the Men of Hell and the rest would fall like dominoes since Romeo had killed the last president in cold blood. This night should have ended with only two men dead—Romeo and Boone. Bandit had assured him of Romeo's inability to rule and Boone's inability to care, but the Men of Hell hadn't fought like a group on the cusp of imploding. They'd fought as a club, together, watching one another's backs.

Bizerk was right. They couldn't wait. Right now, the group was probably divided with some at the hospital and others stuck talking with the cops. It would be relatively easy to infiltrate Bair Memorial and find out where the Men of Hell were being treated because people usually saw two or more bikers and grouped them together. If they took out the wounded men, that would further weaken Romeo's ranks and morale.

"All right," he said and set the bottle of beer on the counter. "We'll do it your way. The fewer men the better, so everyone else get some rest. Tomorrow we'll start rethinking how to get Romeo and Boone."

* * * *

When the ambulance arrived at the emergency entrance, Chloe jumped out of the cab and rushed around to watch the hospital staff take out Wrench. Dr. Pinder looked surprised to see her.

"Victim was shot approximately thirty minutes ago," she told him, completely focused on Wrench's gurney being lowered. "Epigastric area, maybe upper umbilical. The bullet is still inside. I applied sterile gauze and had him hold pressure."

The EMTs began spouting off blood pressure and other vitals, as a weeping Petunia came out of the ambulance last. As soon as she saw Chloe, she wiped her eyes and drew in a deep breath. Chloe gave her a supportive nod before rushing behind Dr. Pinder.

"I would like to scrub in, Doctor," she said as they hurried down the hallway.

"You're not on duty."

"No, but his wife trusts me," she said. "They're my friends."

"All right," Dr. Pinder replied.

Chloe shot off to the locker room to change into scrubs and get the OR prepped. She didn't have a lot of time.

She quickly gathered all the items she thought she might need for an open stomach surgery, including the wrapped sterile instrument cases, before hurrying into the operating room. She saw Susan prepping as well, but ignored her. Her focus lay entirely on helping Wrench. The last thing she wanted to do was have to go out there and tell her new friend that something bad had happened to her husband.

Wrench was put under and the exploratory surgery began. They had to retrieve the bullet and make sure there wasn't any internal bleeding. Several hours later, Dr. Pinder sewed him up, and for the first time, Chloe took a relieved breath behind her mask. Wrench was going to be fine. The bullet had ripped through the top part of his stomach but had missed his spine by centimeters. He'd have to take it easy for a few weeks, and eat squishy foods, but barring anything unforeseen, like a nasty infection, Wrench would make a full recovery. He was damn lucky.

As he was wheeled out, Susan stepped up to her. They'd worked the whole case as civil co-workers, pushing aside any personal difficulties in favor of what was best for the patient. But now, Chloe eyed the nurse and waited for her to say her peace.

"You're a psychopath who has no business dealing with patients," Susan said, her voice a little distorted by the stitches still in her tongue. "But you're a damn good surgical assistant. You have a level head and you cared about this man. I'm going to keep my eye on you and if you do anything to harm someone else, I won't hesitate to write you up. And I don't care if you threaten me or not."

Chloe narrowed her gaze but Susan didn't flinch, although she did swallow nervously. It took guts to say that, and Chloe gave a nod of acknowledgment. Susan turned and left the room, her back ramrod straight.

Chloe couldn't help but smile at the woman's courage. It took balls to stand up to a bully, and Chloe realized her actions had been exactly that. Not nice and definitely not those of someone who had her shit together. She didn't make excuses for her actions, but she knew she needed to work on her anger issues.

The question was—did Romeo and Dax really want her for herself, or for the eroticism she brought to the table? She wasn't stupid. She knew the picture she painted because she'd worked hard to paint that canvas. After her childhood, the last thing she'd wanted to be as an adult was a victim. That word was almost as bad as obsessive. The shrinks had told her that she could be dealing with post-traumatic stress the rest of her life but she'd given them the finger on their suggestions. Perhaps it was time to reevaluate things. She didn't think she could do psychiatrists again, but maybe she should tell Dax and Romeo about her last tangent. Just thinking Nathan's name had shame filling her.

She placed the used equipment into the surgery cart and pushed it to the sterile processing room before heading out to find Petunia. Since it was early in the morning, the hospital was a dark echo of itself, relying on the bare minimum of energy to give the illusion of rest. Of course, a hospital never rested, not fully, and it gave the place a creepy quality she'd never thought about before.

Much to her surprise, Boone and Petunia stood talking with Dr. Pinder. When she walked up to them,

Wrench's old lady reached out and hugged her. It felt odd to have someone so thankful to see her—to have a friend—and it made Chloe's heart flutter with happiness.

"Dr. Pinder tells me I can't see him right now," Petunia said.

Chloe met the doctor's gaze over Petunia's shoulder, and he shook his head.

"He's resting in the post-anesthesia care unit right now," Chloe told her. "The PACU nurses will take excellent care of him."

Petunia pulled back, but held onto Chloe's hands. "Will you look in on him, please? I'd feel better with someone I know checking on him."

"I will," she promised. "I'll do that before I leave for the night, okay? You should go be with your kids. Alleviate their worry."

"Thank you, Chloe." With one more squeeze of her hands, Petunia let her go. She bent and grabbed her purse off a chair. "I'll be back tomorrow, okay?"

"Sounds good. Get some rest."

Chloe watched her friend leave. She glanced at Boone with a raised eyebrow.

"Are you done?" he asked.

"Yeah."

"Then I'll stay until you get dressed and take you back to the compound."

"What about Petunia?"

"Her mom is coming to pick her up."

"Oh. Okay. Well, give me about ten minutes."

He nodded.

She and Dr. Pinder left the waiting room.

"You should become a nurse," Dr. Pinder said. "Or a doctor."

"No," she said, shaking her head. "I don't have the long-term patience to be either. I like helping people, but I don't like the bureaucracy of the medical field. Goodnight, Doctor. Thank you for letting me scrub in with you on this case."

"Anytime, Chloe."

They parted company and she made her way back through the darkened halls to the PACU area. As she turned the corner, she saw two big men wearing leathers up ahead and her insides froze. They weren't Men of Hell members. She knew most of them and these two weren't wearing the MOH cuts. The hair on the back of her neck stood up. She followed them, thankful that her sneakers were silent on the floor.

The hospital had the bare minimum security since it had never had a situation arise where it needed more. Bair wasn't a huge city and the crossroads were a parallel highway heading east and west. Chloe's gut tightened and she knew who these bikers were before she even looked at their faces. Vicious and Bizerk had come to finish off some type of vendetta, and she couldn't waste time trying to find a lone security guard who was probably hanging around some nurses' station.

The two men headed to PACU. She had to protect Wrench. So while they walked to the main entrance, she turned and ran onto the surgery floor, taking a moment to grab a sterile preloaded scalpel from one of the OR rooms. It wasn't much, but it was something.

At the recovery room, she peeked into it from the side window and saw the two nurses huddled together as one man held a gun on them. The other man stood next to a sleeping Wrench. She opened the scalpel package and held it behind her back, then she pushed open the door.

"What do you think you're doing?" she demanded.

The man beside Wrench's bed jerked and spun. She immediately identified him as the man who had been pissed at Shantel's passing. His evil face darkened as he recognized her.

"You!"

He took a step toward her, just as she wanted. Her plan was to lure him out of the room and run like hell. A security guard would be useless, but maybe a fire drill would rouse enough people to spook them out of the hospital.

"No, Bizerk! Finish it," the other man ordered.

Vicious, she presumed.

"Don't you want to hurt the person who killed your precious Shantel?" she taunted. "She was my first kill, you know. I thought I would feel remorse over taking a life, but, surprisingly, it wasn't hard to swallow when it was *that* bitch."

With a roar of rage, Bizerk lunged for her. Chloe was small and quick. She ducked and burst out of PACU, running for all she was worth. Right behind her, heavy footfalls chased her. She might be fast, but he was determined, and a hand grabbed the back of her shirt to halt her. The momentum carried her around, spinning her, and they both went down in a heap of tangled limbs. Chloe slashed with the scalpel and it caught him in the neck, the extremely sharp blade slicing his skin open. Blood splattered across her face. He yowled again and she kneed him right between his thighs. He rolled off her, cradling his groin, and she thought she was free, but the next instant, a hand grabbed her shoulder and she looked up into Vicious' furious face. He smashed a fist into her cheek.

Darkness claimed her.

* * * *

Boone sat in the waiting room, head back, resting. He stared at the ceiling. He'd known what Romeo was going to try to pull right before the shit had hit the fan. It didn't take a genius to figure out he was going to try to abdicate. Dumb fuck. He'd really thought Romeo was made of sterner stuff, then, when the lights went out and the club came under attack, he saw a side of the younger man he'd never seen before.

Romeo had become a leader.

Away from all the shit that clouded his mind, Romeo had instantly assumed the role Wheels had believed was tailor made for him, and damn if he hadn't agreed with the old president in that moment. Perhaps there was hope for the Men of Hell after all.

As he contemplated getting some gross hospital coffee, footsteps rushed by, down the hall, snapping him to attention. He surged to his feet and glanced out of the waiting room, down the darkened corridor, to see two security men running in the direction Chloe had gone. He rolled his eyes. Shit. When was Chloe *not* causing trouble?

He followed. Only, when he got closer, he saw a couple of nurses gesturing, crying, and they screamed when they looked at him. He held up his hands, showing that he wasn't armed.

"I'm waiting for Chloe Matsumoto," he said cautiously. "I'm her ride."

One of the nurses took a deep breath. "They took her."

Ice poured through him. "They *who*?"

"S-some people like you," she whispered, gesturing to his leather cut.

"Bikers?"

She nodded. "One held a gun on us. The other was going to kill the patient. But Chloe... She stepped in. Got them to chase her. She *saved* him. Saved us!"

Oh, shit. Shit!

"Which way did they go?"

The nurse pointed to the emergency exit, and he ran, hoping like hell that he could catch up with them because he did *not* want to make that call to Romeo. The roar of a motorcycle drowned out his thoughts and he spied them peeling out of the parking lot. Chloe's limp body draped the back of one of the men, and Boone wasted no time, running to his bike. He straddled it, started it up and took off after them. His only concern was making sure he kept his eyes on the bikes. If he lost sight of her, there wasn't a doubt in his mind that Chloe wouldn't live much longer.

As Boone pushed harder, the leader glanced over his shoulder and knew that he'd been spotted, although it was ridiculous to think Boone could follow them with stealth. They were on motorcycles, for fuck's sake, and none of them had exhaust baffles, causing sounds to bounce back and forth between the mom-and-pop stores.

The two bikers throttled through town, breaking every speeding law as they wove in and out of the narrow two-lane traffic. He cursed under his breath and mimicked them, hoping that no pedestrian got the stupid idea to cross the street at the wrong time. People stopped and stared, but he ignored everything except the two bikes in front of him. Once they reached the outskirts, he had a vague idea of where the two were heading. He reached into his pocket and pulled out his cell phone to report everything to Romeo.

Chapter Nineteen

Romeo had watched the ambulance, which contained Chloe, Petunia and Wrench, pull out of the compound before turning to the sheriff.

"The logistics of this are a nightmare, Romeo," Sheriff Wilson muttered.

Romeo nodded. The officers swarmed the area while the Men of Hell gathered the dead. None of his men, thank God, because Romeo didn't consider Bandit one of his Brothers anymore. But the Double Guns had lost three, including the man he'd killed.

"Hold on," he told the sheriff. He pulled out his switchblade as he walked over to Bandit's body. He looked at Boone. "Where's his tattoo?"

"Chest."

"Show me."

Gabby used his own knife to remove the cut in pieces. Then he sliced through the clothing and jerked the edges apart to show the Men of Hell symbol inked on his right pectoral. Romeo leaned down and sawed through the muscle, making a mental note to sharpen the blade. Because he was dead, the blood didn't squirt out, but some of it, the stuff still lingering in the capillaries, ran down the torso.

"What the fuck are you doing?" the sheriff demanded.

"This asshole was working for them," Romeo said coldly. "He doesn't get to be buried with the tat. The ink is ours, so I'm taking it back."

"That's mutilation. I can arrest you for that."

Romeo glared at him and, almost immediately, the sheriff backed down. The tattoo was bigger than Cipher's so it took a few extra minutes to get it off. Gabby held out Bandit's cut and Romeo tossed the pile of skin on top of it.

"Burn that," he ordered.

Gabby nodded.

He stared at the men, his Brothers, and something shifted inside him. It dawned on him that these men looked toward him for orders on what to do next, that they accepted him without reserve as their leader — their boss. They would have no hesitation whatsoever doing what he ordered them to do, and suddenly, all the confusion he harbored over the president patch he wore melted away. The mental door opened and all those lectures Wheels had given him sank in, and he knew exactly what needed to be done.

"Sheriff," he said. "This group came onto our turf, attacked us. So I would appreciate your crew cleaning up their carcasses and getting them the hell off my property."

Sheriff Wilson frowned. "But I need statements —"

"Your statement is that they broke the law, not us. We defended ourselves. And you tell everyone in Bair the Men of Hell will protect them too. This is our town, and we protect what's ours. Understood?"

Slowly, the sheriff nodded.

Romeo spun, already dismissing him. He pointed to Boone. "Someone needs to be with Wrench. Go to the hospital."

"On it," Boone replied.

Romeo looked at Dax. "Tell me how they got in."

"Bandit volunteered for sentinel duty and at some point he knocked Johnny, the other man on duty, out. Then he unbolted the gate, cut the power and went to the backup generator. Only Wrench managed to get the drop on him."

"One man nearly brought us down because he was still smarting over Shepard." Romeo shook his head bitterly. "Who do you think still poses a threat to us?"

Dax took a moment to glance around, eyeing each member. He shook his head. "No one, Rome."

"I have to trust everyone, Dax. That's how this works. You trust the Brothers or this club goes down in flames."

"I know."

"Then we need to talk to all the members," Romeo said. "I want to hear each oath of loyalty. It's time to stop dancing around Shepard's ghost."

"All right."

Satisfied, Romeo moved on to the next order of business—seeing the women and making sure they were all okay. In the past, the Men of Hell hadn't been very accommodating toward the old ladies, and that was another step he planned on changing. The hours passed by as he worked with the men and women to clean up the clubhouse, making sure to talk with each person. He knew each man, having been patched in before them all. He'd been thirteen when he had landed there and each person had a journey. Some shared, some kept it to themselves, but that night he learned a lot more about where they were all heading.

The children had passed out long ago, sleeping in the bunker with people taking turns keeping watch over them. He'd never been so thankful in his life that he'd listened to his gut telling him to get everyone to safety.

There came a point during the long night when people couldn't go on. The place had been pretty much put back to rights, except for the shot-out windows and the bullet holes in the wood that painted a very grim reminder. Their lives would never be white picket fences and rose gardens, but as Romeo looked around, he knew he wouldn't have it any other way. This was his life, this was his home...his town...and he loved it. Deciding to get some rest, he was halfway up to his room when his cell phone went off. Boone's name appeared on the screen. An update on Wrench, no doubt.

"Yeah?"

"She was taken!"

Romeo halted. "Chloe?"

"Yeah," Boone yelled through the phone. The sound of his bike was almost deafening through the connection. "I was waiting for her when all hell broke loose. Nurses in the recovery unit said two bikers came in, held a gun on them and threatened to kill Wrench when Chloe came in and distracted them. She *saved* Wrench, Romeo. But she was taken."

What the hell!

They hadn't even recovered from what had happened earlier this night...morning...whatever. Pre-dawn light glazed the eastern skyline, letting him know he'd been up almost twenty-four hours.

"Are you there?" Boone demanded.

"Yeah. Thinking. Chloe killed Shantel in self-defense but Bizerk... Shit, he's going to want revenge."

"I'm following them. When I heard, I ran outside and saw them. They had to bungee cord her to one of them. She's out cold."

Romeo was already moving to his bike. "Where are you?"

"Outside of town. Shit, I think we're heading toward—"

The sound of gunfire blasted through the call. The line went dead. Romeo stared at the phone in his hand. He dialed Boone, but the call went straight to voicemail. Fear punched him right in the heart. Chloe had been taken by the very man who wanted her dead.

And he had no idea where she was.

Chapter Twenty

Boone flinched as Vicious turned and shot at him. He dropped his cell. He didn't need to follow them anymore. He knew exactly where Vicious and Bizerk were heading. Bandit's trailer home. The fucking traitor had allowed these assholes to stay in his home.

Boone turned off onto a road, bypassing the mobile park, deciding to give them a false sense of security. He drove around the perimeter until he found a good place to stash his bike, in a grove of trees where no one would fuck with it. After pulling his gun out from its holster, he checked to make sure it was loaded and the safety was off before he moved into the trailer park.

Dawn was breaking, making it easier for him to maneuver through the neighbors' yards. It didn't take long to find Bandit's home, and he counted six bikes. Vicious' and Bizerk's, which left four other members. Boone shook his head. Dumb fucks, taking on a fully functioning motorcycle club with what? Ten members, including the dead at their compound? They must have really thought Bandit was going to come through for them.

He hurried up to one window and looked through the cracked curtains. The kitchen lay at the front of the trailer, the living room in the middle, with a hallway extending into the back that he presumed led to the bedrooms. Bizerk slapped Chloe awake and the little hellcat came up swinging. Boone grinned until Bizerk backhanded her, knocking her to the ground. She cradled her face and stared at her kidnapper, and if looks could kill, no doubt the man would have been eviscerated in seconds. He didn't know Chloe all that well, but he knew enough to know that she wasn't someone to fuck with.

The other members, galvanized into action, brought out their arsenal of weapons, mostly rifles and 9 millimeters. What he wouldn't have done for a flash grenade right now.

He continued to watch them, trying to figure out their weak spots. A movement from Chloe caught his attention. She braced herself on the floor then swiped one foot out, catching Bizerk right at his ankles in a sharp, swift kick. The man may have been bigger and stronger, but she hit him directly on his bone and he went down.

Damn. She was little but she knew right where to get people. Whoever had taught her taught her well. In one smooth, flawless maneuver, she immediately jumped onto Bizerk's back and managed to roll with him, his back to her front. He became her shield so no one could shoot her. She also managed to get her hand on his gun, although he was beginning to regain his stunned senses. Boone figured that this was a good time to help her. He hurried to the front door and, with one heavy kick, broke it open. He ducked to the side as gunfire erupted.

He waited until there was a pause and quickly popped around to shoot twice then ducked back to safety. Despite Chloe having her human shield, he didn't want to risk hitting her. There were two shots from inside then another lull. He dared to peek inside and saw that Chloe had managed to get her hands on Bizerk's gun. She crouched behind a chair, aiming it steadily. Bizerk wasn't there, but he couldn't have gone far in a trailer. Boone cautiously entered, pointing his gun out, surveying the scene. Two men lay on the ground, dead. The rest of the men were nowhere to be seen.

"Where did they go, Chloe?"

"Boone?" she asked, surprised. She glanced from behind the chair and slowly stood. "I got two of them."

"I see that," he replied and made his way over to her. "Where are Bizerk and Vicious?"

"Ran down the hallway, I think. All of them."

"There's a back door," he said. "This was Bandit's trailer."

She nodded.

He moved slowly toward the hallway, mindful of an ambush. Chloe walked toward the kitchen, and he was thankful that she knew how to handle a gun. This was an environment he knew, the hunting of men, and he had absolutely no fear. His weapon was an extension of his arm. Every sense was on the alert for movement or sounds. Still, he was surprised when the front door banged open.

"Boone!" Chloe cried.

He spun and fired. Bizerk's gun went off at the same time, but Boone didn't flinch as the bullet struck the paneling beside his head. His aim, however, had been true. Blood welled from the gaping hole directly over Bizerk's heart and Bizerk crumpled to the ground, lifeless.

Boone walked over to the man and kicked him to make sure he wouldn't be getting up. The dull eyes staring into nothing confirmed it. He never liked taking a life, but he didn't hesitate when it was self-defense, or as a way of protecting someone. He'd not only saved Chloe, he'd saved the club.

"Watch out!" Chloe cried.

The click of her empty chamber registered right before he spun to see her throw herself in front of Vicious, who had come from one of the bedrooms, and wrestle with the gun he held. The echoing blast as it went off reverberated around the interior, seemingly louder than when he'd pulled the trigger on Bizerk.

For a timeless moment, no one moved. Then Vicious practically tossed her to Boone and she fell into his arms, clutching the man's gun. With her bulk, he couldn't aim correctly at Vicious' retreating back.

"I'll get you," Vicious vowed, screaming over his shoulder as he ran.

Then he was gone, down the hall, presumably to the back door. Seconds later, a motorcycle roared away. Boone tried to set Chloe aside, but she wasn't cooperating with him. She just lay like a lump against him. Vicious' gun fell from her hands to clatter to the floor.

"Chloe?" he asked. The warm trickle of something oozed over his hand. He shook her and her head flopped back, her black hair sliding to reveal her closed eyes and pale features. Blood ran from her mouth, and when he held up his hand, it was covered with warm serum.

"Oh, no," he whispered. "Shit! Chloe! Don't you fucking die on me!"

He shoved his gun back into the holster under his cut and swung her up in his arms. By the time he stepped out of the trailer, some of the neighbors had ventured out of their homes to see what was going on.

"I need a car!" he yelled

No one said a word, just stared at him as if he spoke gibberish.

"God damn it! She's dying! Help me," he ordered harshly.

A teenager stepped forward. "Yeah, come on. I'll drive you to the hospital."

Boone nodded his thanks and followed him, hoping to God that she wouldn't die on the way.

Chapter Twenty-One

Suffocation.
Immobility.
Fright.
Chloe thrashed about, water flowing over her head and trapping her in the black abyss. She couldn't breathe, couldn't escape, and little by little her sanity fled while panic took root.

Her eyes were wide open as she twisted, trying to find release from the dark oblivion beckoning her, trying to find some light to guide her. But there was nothing to rescue her, no place to find sanctuary. The dark was endless and it pulled her down.

Her last thought was to scream out her frustration.
She opened her mouth, felt the water rush in...

Chloe fluttered her eyelids open once, twice, blinking away the double vision until the ceiling she stared at came into focus. Pain itched at her subconscious and it hurt to breathe. But it was the antiseptic smell and the beep, beep, beep of a heart monitor that alerted her to the fact that she lay in a hospital bed. Slowly, she turned her head. The oxygen cannula tube under her nose crunched a little as she realized she was a patient. Then the reason why she was a patient came rushing back into her memory, causing her to gasp.

A body filled her line of view and she glanced up to see a worried expression filling Romeo's face. Dax squeezed in behind him, and she smiled faintly at both of them.

"Do I look as bad as I feel?" she whispered.

Romeo ran a gentle finger over her cheek. If memory served correctly, the same cheek Bizerk had hit.

"You're going to be all right," Dax answered.

"How's Boone?"

"He owes you," Romeo said. "You saved his life."

"I'm sure he saved me too, by getting me to the hospital."

She shifted a little and grimaced at the pain. Not much, which surprised her, and she flicked a look at the pain pump next to her bed. Morphine. No wonder Romeo liked the stuff. She licked her lips, and Dax must have sensed her thirst, because he reached for the cup and pitcher on the table in the corner. A second later, he held a straw up to her lips and she sucked in cool, refreshing water. Her scratchy throat eased.

"Where was I shot?"

"Right lung," Romeo replied. "Lower lobe. You've been out for a day and a half."

She'd had a patient once who'd been shot in a lung. He hadn't made it, so Chloe was extremely happy that she hadn't followed his fate. Her mind automatically went through the procedures that would have been done. An endotracheal had probably been administered, which accounted for the rough feeling in her throat. Somewhere on her right side was a chest tube, no doubt, draining the fluid from her damaged lung. She wondered if Susan had been the OR nurse during the surgery to repair the damage and remove the bullet.

Oh, the irony.

IVs dripped antibiotics and nutrients into her veins, and she knew she probably looked like death warmed over. But Romeo and Dax stared at her with relief in their eyes. She raised her hands toward them, and each man took hold of one, holding tight. She drifted back to sleep, content.

* * * *

The next time she opened her eyes, her grandfather stood at the foot of her bed. The light outside the window announced that she'd slept through the night. She blinked, hoping he was just a figment of her nightmare, but he stayed. His regal features were a cold mask as he surveyed her from head to toe.

"You assured me you could care for Kaiya," he said in Japanese. "And yet I find you unable to care for yourself."

She sighed. She so didn't want to deal with him right now. "I got shot in the lung and you wish to hash this out now?"

He stared at her.

She rolled her eyes.

"Fine," she continued. "I didn't shoot myself, Grandfather. Besides, I saved a man."

"Another one of your obsessions?"

"No," she muttered. "But thanks for always throwing that in my face."

"Can you really blame me when I've had to bail you out of trouble twice?"

She compressed her lips into a flat line. They always went around in circles with this. "Is Kaiya here?"

"She is in the waiting room," he replied. "I'm determining if she should leave with me and go back to Los Angeles."

"Don't be stubborn. Kaiya needs to be out from under your thumb."

He gave a type of deep-chested growl. "Every time someone has stepped away from my thumb, as you put it, it always ends badly. In the course of my life, I've lost my wife to rivals, my son to his hate-filled wife, my daughter and son-in-law to a drunk driver. I almost lost my deaf granddaughter to a human trafficking ring and my other granddaughter to mental demons."

"Don't forget the bullet in the lung." She couldn't help the sarcastic comment rolling off her tongue. Sarcasm was her defense mechanism.

He leveled a dark glare on her. "Do *not* try to be humorous."

"Sorry," she said, although she wasn't the least bit sorry. "But, Grandfather, your life is all about crime. I grew up knowing the violence under the thin veneer of civility you exude, so don't blow smoke up my ass and be offended because I was shot saving a man. Not when your body count touches the heavens. Did you bring the money and the guns?"

He nodded, once.

"Then we're done," she said wearily. "I forgive you, all right? I forgive you for the circumstances that made me as I am. All I wish for now is to never see you again."

"Family is important—"

At that moment, the door opened and one of her grandfather's men stood guard, holding back a very pissed off looking Romeo and Dax.

"Move the hell out of our way!" Romeo growled. "That's our old lady."

Her grandfather nodded, and the guard stepped aside, allowing them to enter. Dax shoved the bodyguard with his shoulder in a manly confrontational way as he passed. Boone pushed in after them.

"They are my family now," Chloe said. She switched to English so the men could understand. "This man is Hiro Matsumoto. My grandfather. He's come to deliver the guns, money and the new club accountant."

"Say what?" Boone demanded.

"I got you an accountant, Boone. You needed someone competent to do your books so I found you the perfect person."

"Wait, Chloe," Romeo said. "Not just anyone can be a treasurer for the club. Our finances aren't exactly — "

"She's my cousin," Chloe said. "Kaiya knows what the family business means, as well as the importance of silence."

Boone shook his head. "If she blabs her mouth, it's all over — for all of us."

"She's deaf." She raised an eyebrow. "Start learning sign language."

"I don't know if I want her to stay with such men," Hiro said in Japanese.

"English," she told him. "And of course Kaiya is staying."

They stared at each another, and for a moment, she remembered those long forgotten Japanese traditions, dressed in a traditional *kimono* gown, participating in the tea ceremony *sado* and listening to the musical chime of a *biwa*. That was a lifetime ago, and she was no longer that type of Japanese girl. Her gaze met Romeo's. Her future now lay with the Men of Hell, and the two men who had managed to capture her affection. Did she love them? It was really too soon to tell, but she knew it wouldn't be long until they were completely ingrained in her heart. This was nothing at all like Nathan.

"These men are what you want?" her grandfather asked in English.

Without taking her eyes off Romeo and Dax, she nodded.

Hiro sighed. "As you wish. *Mou osoi node watashi wa kaeri masu. Watashi wa kore de shitsurei shimasu.*"

It's getting late, I must be going now. Excuse me for leaving first.

Out of nowhere, tears welled up in her eyes. He'd said the traditional Japanese goodbye phrases. She wiped at the wetness on her cheek, hoping like mad that she was having an allergic reaction to something. That was preferable than having feelings for the old man who had chosen his dynasty over his family.

"*O-ki wo tsukete,*" she whispered. *Take care of yourself.*

He nodded once more, turned and left. The door swished closed softly behind him.

"That sounded like a goodbye," Dax said.

She wiped the tears from the corners of her eyes. "It was."

"Is that what you want?" Romeo asked.

"I both love and hate that man."

She looked at Boone, wanting a private moment with her men, and, thankfully, the big guy gave an understanding nod and departed.

"After my bodyguard and unexpected stay in the nuthouse, I thought I had my obsessive tendencies under control," she said. "But my last tangent was over a doctor I worked with, named Nathan. He would talk to me during surgical procedures and tell me how horrible his wife was. Feed on my sympathy in an attempt to seduce me. And it worked. We'd have quick, hot moments of sex in the sleep rooms reserved for doctors working double shifts. Unfortunately for him, I had my little limerence problem."

"What happened?" Romeo asked.

"I thought he was in love with me," she replied. She hated to admit just how stupid she had been. "I thought he needed me. It was my bodyguard all over again. When he told me she wouldn't sign the divorce papers so we could be together, I… I took matters into my own hand. I kidnapped her. Tied her up. Threatened her unless she signed. That's when I found out there weren't any divorce papers. She was a completely innocent woman, and I was the biggest fool on the planet — again."

"The fucker," Dax muttered.

Chloe flashed him a thankful smile.

"I was arrested," she said. "Fired. But before they could prosecute, my grandfather showed up and persuaded Nathan and his wife to drop the charges."

"Persuaded?" Dax questioned.

"In a purely monetary way, of course," she said sarcastically. "Once again, I was institutionalized, then he brought me back to his home while I *recuperated* from my ordeal. It was while I was staying with him that I discovered the file he had on you, Romeo, and the Men of Hell. And that is all of me. Every single ugly scar."

Dax lifted her hand without the IV hooked up, and kissed the back of it. Romeo leaned over and kissed her lightly on the lips.

"No, baby," he said. "No ugly scars at all."

* * * *

Boone exited Chloe's room after the old man and watched as he walked regally down the hallway. Yakuza mafia were a lot more refined than he'd thought. Matsumoto stopped briefly at the entrance to the waiting room before bowing. Then he was gone, two bodyguards following in his wake.

When he approached the room where Gabby waited for him, he heard his taciturn friend laugh. At least he *thought* it was a laugh. He'd not heard Gabby laugh in so long he'd forgotten the sound. Most people thought Gabby couldn't talk, but the truth was, he was deaf in one ear and many times he simply didn't hear what was being said. He was also afraid that his speech wasn't as crystal clear as it used to be and he was afraid of what people thought. His friend had suffered much in the past, but he'd saved Boone's life, and Boone owed his friend everything.

Boone peeked into the room and saw him signing to a young Japanese woman sitting demurely next to him. She was tall, very thin, with a face so angelic it made him want to weep. Out of nowhere, a fist punched him in his gut, and all his breath exited in a whoosh. She turned her almond-shaped eyes his way, so dark and fathomless that he almost drowned in them, and his heart thundered away. He didn't know what to think or say. He just stared at her like a big dumb ass.

"Her name is Kaiya," Gabby said, his rich baritone scratchy from disuse.

Boone had the oddest feeling that he'd fallen, although he wasn't sure in which direction. And he wondered when he would find his equilibrium again.

Chapter Twenty-Two

"You should be resting," Kaiya signed as they approached the entrance to Wheels' house.

Chloe had been out of the hospital for over a month now, which meant six weeks of being coddled as if she was made of spun glass, constantly being asked how she felt, and worst of all...no sex. Instead, she, Dax and Romeo had talked. Hours and hours spent getting to know each other.

"And you need to be out of the hotel." She changed the subject, knowing perfectly well that her cousin would read her lips. Her lung had inflated nicely without any sign of infection and she grew stronger every day. But enough was enough, damn it.

She put the key in the lock and turned the knob. The door swished open with a small creak. Nothing some oil couldn't fix, but she figured it wouldn't bother Kaiya one way or another. Chloe wasn't being crass. That's just how it was.

The sound of bikes rumbled over the suburban landscape and Chloe glanced down the street. It only took a moment for Romeo, Dax, Boone and Gabby to cruise into sight. Chloe rolled her eyes and nudged her cousin, thumbing at the men who pulled up into the driveway. This was getting ridiculous. She couldn't even pee by herself anymore.

"You are in a relationship with two men," Kaiya said in sign.

Chloe frowned, wondering where this conversation was heading. "Yeah. So?"

"Do you think Boone and Gabby are open to the same arrangement?"

"What?" Chloe asked sharply. "Why?"

Kaiya was the epitome of virginal purity. Her face, her bearing, her eyes... She had always been the calm one. The good girl. Hell, for a long time Chloe thought her cousin bathed in holy water every day just to hold onto her angelic disposition.

"Because I want them."

Chloe blinked, for once at a loss for words. Her cousin wanted not one but *two* men? Did she even have a clue what that meant? What it entailed? These were men, not boys, and they would expect things to be down and dirty. She shot a quick glance at Gabby, seeing his scar and imagining what had to have happened to leave such a mark. Boone was tough, but Gabby was cold.

"Uh, do you know what it means to be with two men, sweetie?"

Kaiya gave her a no-shit look. "I'm not a virgin, although I think you think I am."

Chloe opened her mouth to say something about that stunning revelation. What the hell did Kaiya mean about *not* being a virgin? But before she could ask her question, the men walked up, effectively shutting down her shock. But this wasn't over. Chloe was very determined to find out who'd had the audacity to defile her baby cousin. The horrible thought that she might have been raped during her abduction settled in the pit of her stomach and burned like acid.

"So," Romeo said. "You're going to transform Wheels' house?"

Chloe shrugged. "Seemed like a good place for Kaiya to live."

He and Dax shared a glance.

"Just Kaiya, right?" Romeo asked.

She folded her arms over her chest. "That's right. I *am* your old lady, although I do take exception to being called old. I'm only twenty-eight, you know."

Dax settled his arms on her hips. She licked her lips and his gaze was instantly drawn to where she deliberately dipped her tongue out. It had been six weeks, a lifetime, and she was feeling perfectly fine. Tonight was the night she was going to have both her men. She'd been prepping her ass long enough.

But first, she had to make sure Kaiya was okay. She leaned up and kissed Dax on the lips before turning to face her cousin. What she wanted to say she didn't want the other men to know, so she signed.

"Were you raped when you were abducted?"

Her cousin looked steadily at her, giving nothing away. Serene. Calm. They might be completely opposite in temperament, but Chloe loved her unconditionally. And if anyone hurt Kaiya, she would take the person apart, extremity by extremity.

"Go be with your men, Chloe," Kaiya signed back. "I have my own."

Then Kaiya linked an arm through Gabby's and Boone's and entered the house, dismissing her. Chloe had half a mind to chase her down and demand the truth, but Romeo laid a restraining hand on her arm.

"I don't know what you two said, but she seems okay being with Boone and Gabby."

"They'll take care of her, sweetheart," Dax added. "Come on. Let's go for a ride."

She let them lead her over to their bikes and she decided to ride with Romeo. They'd only been on a few short rides during the month and a half—nothing too strenuous, mainly going to the doctor for checkups—but she loved the freedom the bikes allowed. No doors, nothing to hinder the heat of the sun burning down. Romeo handed her the helmet he'd bought her not too long ago, and she strapped it on before slipping on a pair of sunglasses. Romeo got on his bike and she straddled behind him, hiking her feet up to a safe shelf. As they roared down the street, she snuggled up behind him, holding tightly.

There wasn't much to Nebraska, she had to admit. Lots of sweeping plains with corn or some other crop growing, all swaying in one direction with the wind. The horizon went on for miles, green land and bright blue skies. Puffs of clouds hung like fluffy cotton balls. The peaceful picturesque view belied the violence that had happened not that long ago. This land was completely different from the grind of Los Angeles, but surprisingly she didn't miss it at all.

They eventually made their way back to the compound. Romeo had implemented some changes. The ease with which the so-called Double Guns had broken through their defenses had initiated a type of overhaul. Each floodlight had its own backup generator, so if one went down, the others weren't incapacitated. The house had several security measures in place, including bulletproof shielding that rolled down with a flick of a switch. The sense of stability had convinced the rest of the club to accept her money. Motorcycle clubs were notoriously paternalistic, not to mention full of testosterone-fueled pride. She'd eventually talked them into taking it as a loan, with Romeo's promise to return the money as the club sold the drugs. Boone and Gabby were scheduled any day to leave for the Canadian border and meet up with Red Eye.

They'd even made strides in the public eye, donating fireworks for the Fourth of July celebration and mingling with folks. Romeo wanted their presence known and accepted, as they would be watching out for their town from now on. A positive presence, rather than an unwelcome blight. It was slow going, but it was a step in the right direction.

She was fully moved into the compound, and had paid to have the room next to theirs converted into an extention. If the three of them were going to be living together, then she insisted on some additional space. They had upgraded to a California king-sized bed to make it comfortable for them all to sleep. As soon as they walked into the room, she turned and beckoned both men with a finger.

"Something you want, Miss Matsumoto?" Dax asked teasingly.

"I've been wearing a butt plug long enough, so yes, there is something I want, Daxton Squire," she replied sassily.

"Jesus, woman," Romeo murmured. He cupped his erection straining against his jeans. "It's been too long since I've been buried in that pussy. Stop teasing me."

She pushed his hand aside and massaged his hard-on through the material. "It's been too long because you wouldn't touch me."

"You were shot in the lung," Dax reminded her. "Not exactly conducive to a marathon sexcapade."

"Oh, I like the sound of that." She snagged a loop on Dax's waist and pulled him close until both men sandwiched her. She glanced back and forth between him and Romeo speculatively. "Which one wants my pussy and which one wants my ass?"

"Shit, woman, you can't say stuff like that or I'm going to come in my jeans," Romeo muttered.

She stood on tiptoe and licked his lips. "Get undressed. Now."

They obeyed, although she had a suspicious feeling that they would be dealing out their own brand of retribution for her ordering them about. It made her pussy even wetter to think about them punishing her for her impertinence.

When they were naked, they walked around her still-clothed body, studying her. She had to admit it was hot, having them look her over, judge her in a purely sexual manner. Her breath came in jerky little spurts and her heart thundered with the sweetest anticipation. Waiting. What were they going to say to her?

"Unbutton your shirt."

Romeo's order had her hand shaking as she hurried to comply, fumbling as she pushed the small buttons through the holes. They didn't touch her, but they didn't need to. God, her pussy was dripping, so she clenched her thighs together to alleviate some of the ache.

"Legs apart, Chloe," Dax said, slapping her ass. "You will not get yourself off, do you hear me? It will only be Rome or myself making you come. Understand?"

She nodded, biting her lip to hold back the moan.

"Now take off your shirt," he instructed. "And your bra."

She slid her arms out and let the shirt fall somewhere behind her. Dax just watched as she reached behind her back to undo the clasp of the bra. It came free, proudly displaying her small breasts. Really, she didn't need to wear one, but she liked the sense of security a bra offered. But it seemed like Dax and Romeo didn't mind that she wasn't more endowed because their focus centered like laser points on her breasts. Her nipples beaded, aching buds that desperately wanted to be sucked.

"Very nice," Dax said approvingly. Then he bent his head to kiss first one breast then the other.

Chloe couldn't help thrusting out her chest, and he obliged, closing his teeth to nip then suck until her nipples were slick with his saliva.

"You like that, don't you?" Romeo asked, his breath fanning into her ear as he nibbled the lobe. "You like having Dax milk your little titties?"

She could only nod since Romeo had decided to divest her of her pants. He reached around her slim waist and unbuttoned her jeans. Then he slid his hands under the material and pushed down, ridding her hips of the material until the jeans pooled at her ankles. He'd snagged her panties along the way then helped her remove all of the clothing from her body. She was now naked in front of them, panting. Wanting. God, how she wanted.

"Get on all fours," he ordered.

Dax stopped his assault on her breasts and stepped back. She took a deep breath, hoping to calm her frantically beating heart, and wiggled her ass as she got on the bed as he'd asked, on hands and knees.

A hand gripped her thigh, and the rough callus on the palm brought all her nerve endings to attention. It glided up over her ass cheek, and a body settled behind her — Romeo.

"Spread your legs."

Once again, she did as he'd commanded and spread them as far as possible. The position opened her sex for his viewing pleasure, made her vulnerable, and it was the only time she willingly turned over complete control to someone else. Not even with Nathan had she given that up.

The bed in front of her dipped, and a long, thick cock appeared in her line of vision. Dax speared his fingers through her hair and brought her mouth toward him, telling without words what he wanted. Chloe leaned forward and kissed the tip, letting her tongue slid through the hole to catch the pre-cum dripping from it. Dax was salty, bitter, but addictive. She encircled her lips around the head and he let out an appreciative groan.

"Oh yeah, sweetheart," Dax said. "Suck my fucking cock. Take it deep."

As he held her by the hair, he withdrew, his dick glistening wet with her saliva. Chloe loved the dirty talk, loved how the words made her feel naughty. Dax returned her mouth to his dick, guiding her. He pumped in and out in a steady rhythm as she passively let him use her lips for his own pleasure. She didn't mind. It was a heady feeling knowing that she was a vessel that he enjoyed. A toy. He held her head with both hands as he fucked her face.

But it wasn't just her face that was being played with. Behind her, Romeo twisted the butt plug then pulled it free of her ass. She'd gotten used to the feeling of being full and the loss had her moaning.

"She's so fucking wet," Romeo exclaimed, rubbing his fingers against the folds of her pussy. He didn't penetrate, so she wiggled her hips, hoping he'd get the hint to sink inside her, but all he gave her was a smack on a butt cheek. Fire licked through her and she wiggled again, hoping for more. He didn't disappoint.

"Oh, you like a little spanking, do you?" Romeo asked.

He smacked her ass again, this time moving to the opposite cheek. Four more times he spanked, and each time her pussy dripped a little more until she was writhing in need.

"Careful, sweetheart," Dax said and eased out of her mouth. A string of saliva connected them from her mouth to his tip. It dangled for a moment then broke. "You were working her up so much her teeth were coming out."

Romeo stopped the smacks and he swiped one finger along her cunt lips again. This time, however, he pushed farther and stroked her slit. Chloe knew she was completely drenched — and hot — and she desperately needed something more than a finger.

"Please," she whispered.

"Please what?" Romeo murmured.

"Fill me up."

She squirmed her hips, then his finger was gone. The bed dipped a little, then his tongue pushed into her pussy to tease her opening. While Romeo tasted and teased her, Dax kissed her neck. Then he scooted until he slid under her and kissed in a straight line down her to her tits. He licked her areolae and made tiny wet circles, eventually nibbling on her nipples until they were aching points that had her clit pulsing.

When Romeo gently clamped down on her swollen clit, it was too much and she shattered with a little scream. Wave after wave of pleasure burned through her body until she was left weak and trembling.

"Oh, yeah," Romeo said as he withdrew his mouth.

Chloe still panted from her climax and tried desperately to regain some of her senses. "She's ready for us."

Dax abruptly pulled away from her breasts and left her. Without his body to support her, she almost collapsed. But before she fully realized what was happening, he had settled beside her and captured her around the waist to draw her legs over his hips. She stared down into his handsome face.

"You know what me and Romeo did while you were recuperating?" he asked.

She blinked. He wanted to *talk* to her right now? She could barely wrap her brain around words so she shook her head.

"We got ourselves tested, made sure we were clean," he answered.

Then he grabbed her hips and pushed her down while he surged up, and slid his cock into her without resistance. Her moan of blissful acceptance became lost as his mouth found hers and he kissed her.

He gripped her tightly as he fucked her hard and fast, working his cock deeper into her body. She tried to push back, to reciprocate, but his speed only allowed her to hang on and enjoy the ride.

"Your pussy is so fucking tight," he managed to say between grunts. "Holy fuck, I'm so deep inside you. So good. So fucking good."

He surged once more and held her still. He didn't come, and Chloe wondered why he wasn't moving, until she felt hands pry apart her ass, and lube dribbled down the crack. A finger brushed over her back hole.

"I'm going to take your ass now, baby," Romeo said. "I'm wearing a condom. It's cleaner. But the next time I take your pussy, I'll be able to feel all of you."

His words had her squirming.

"Fuck me," she panted. "Please. Fuck me now."

"Slide out a little, Dax," Romeo said.

Dax did as he'd asked.

Every nerve ending in her pussy throbbed with anticipation.

"Now, I'm going to fuck this tight ass, Chloe. You'll belong to both of us. Our little pussy girl."

"Yes," she whispered. "Yes. Take me."

More lube dribbled down, then he leaned over her. He held her ass open as the blunt tip of his cock touched her anus. Chloe pushed out as he breached the tight ring of muscle, helping him inside. It burned, but it wasn't painful since she'd prepped her asshole, and the burn only drove her lust higher. He slid in just a little then pulled out, added more lube and pushed back in. With him in the back and Dax in the front, she was stuffed full. It was tight and just a little uncomfortable, so she mentally relaxed her muscles even more.

"That's it, baby," Romeo said. "God, I can feel you, Dax. Through her, I can feel you."

"Holy shit, she's tight," Dax muttered.

"Pull out some more. Let me slide in, then, when I pull out, you go in."

They worked in tandem, learning how to operate, and soon they were a well-oiled machine. As one slid in, the other pulled out, fucking her until she was nothing but a big ball of sensation.

"Oh, my fucking God!" Chloe managed to say, although how she was still capable of speech was beyond her.

"I see my dick sliding into your ass, and I feel Dax fucking your pussy," Romeo said. "Jesus, that's fucking hot."

"Holy shit, Rome, her cunt is so tight," Dax replied. "I don't think I'm going to last much longer."

"Faster," she gasped. "Harder. Please!"

The orgasm climbed quickly within her. It wouldn't be long before she hurtled toward ecstasy. It had never been like this before, this intense, this *full*. It was beyond reason, beyond normal pleasure. Dax reached down and pinched her clit, and that had her spiraling out into the heavens as she exploded into a pure, perfect moment of nirvana, like timelessness after jumping before gravity took control.

"Oh, fuck," Dax moaned. He buried himself deep in her body as he found his release. Hot cum bathed her insides as he jerked out of control with each jet. His body shook under her right before he collapsed.

When Dax was spent, Romeo wrapped a hand on her shoulder and surged hard and fast, chasing his own plateau.

"Yes!" he cried.

She felt him swell in her ass.

"Oh, Chloe, yes!"

Then his cock slipped out of her body and he collapsed onto his side, next to where she lay on top of Dax. They were all breathing heavily, and Chloe reveled in the glorious orgasm as well as having her two men near.

* * * *

She must have fallen asleep because when she woke up, shadows touched the corners of the room. Dax had an arm snuggled around her waist while Romeo's leg kept hers captive. She moved slightly, and their grips tightened.

"Are you awake?" Dax asked softly.

"I am now."

Romeo groaned a little and turned on his back, freeing her legs. "You wore me out," he told her.

She ran a hand down his sculptured torso, over his hard abs to grab his erection. "I think it missed me."

Romeo snagged her and pulled her up onto his cock. He must have cleaned up before going to sleep because there wasn't a condom, but she was still nice and wet from their activity. She sank down effortlessly.

"Ride me, love," he said.

So she did, taking her time now that the fevered frenzy from earlier was gone. Dax presented his cock to her mouth and she sucked him in. She could spend every day in bed with her men, loving them and being loved by them. Every fantasy fulfilled. When Dax spurted in her mouth, she drank him down. After that, she and Romeo found fulfillment in each other's arms.

They cuddled together as the shadows faded to night. Their stomachs growled with hunger, but Chloe was loath to leave the bubble they'd created.

"This is it for me, Chloe," Romeo said, stroking her hair. "No more other pussy. Just yours."

Somehow, the darkness eased the pressure of talking about commitment. She smiled.

"You're saying you'll be faithful?"

"Yes."

"Good. Because you know I have a slight problem with sharing."

Dax chuckled. "What about me?"

"You'd better be faithful too, or I'll shoot the bitch in the kneecaps. I'm a crack shot, remember?"

"Oh, I remember," Dax replied. "As long as it's only me and Rome, I don't care if you stalk us."

"I'll hold you to that," she said.

"And, Chloe?" Dax asked. "I think I love you."

"Yeah," Romeo added. "What he said."

Her heart thumped with happiness as her insides went all warm and gooey. "Well, that's good. I think I love you both too. But we'll have to have lots more sex to make sure."

Romeo laughed and bent to kiss her.

Epilogue

Vicious stood in the shade of a large oak tree, staring at the man who had taken everything from him. His hopes, his heart were completely destroyed. He'd wanted his own club, with his love beside him. But Bizerk was dead and Boone Tempest was the reason.

The other men he'd collected had scattered, running back to their old club in Omaha, no doubt relaying the sad tale of how the Men of Hell had kicked their asses. The MOH had now become a formidable club that many would think twice about crossing. Everything he'd planned for and worked hard to achieve was gone.

Something snapped inside him as he stared at Boone. The need for vengeance clawed at his insides. Boone got on his bike, his ever-present shadow, Gabby, beside him. A young girl got on the back of Gabby's bike and held on tight as they zoomed away from the house.

Perhaps Boone's big silent friend was the way to avenge Bizerk. Retribution would be slow, prolonged, but find it he would. He just had to wait for the right opportunity.

About the Author

I like writing about the very ordinary girl thrust into extraordinary circumstances, so my heroines will probably never be lawyers, doctors or corporate high rollers. I try to write characters who aren't cookie cutters and push myself to write complicated situations that I have no idea how to resolve, forcing me to think outside the box. I love writing characters who are real, complex and full of flaws, heroes and heroines who find redemption through love.

I've been pretty fortunate in life to experience some amazing things. I've lived in France, traveled throughout Europe, Australia and New Zealand. I am a mom to an amazing little boy. I'm surrounded by friends and family. And although I love holding a book in my hand, I absolutely adore my e-reader, which I've named Ruby. I love to hear from readers so I've made it really easy to find me on the web.

Beth D. Carter loves to hear from readers. You can find her contact information, website and author biography at http://www.totallybound.com.

TOTALLY
BOUND

Home of Erotic Romance

www.ingramcontent.com/pod-product-compliance
Lightning Source LLC
Chambersburg PA
CBHW020415180626
46812CB00003B/989